SCENE CITY

SCENE CITY

A Novel

By Róisín Tapponi

VERSO

London • New York

All resemblance to actual persons, including the first-person singular, is purely coincidental.

First published by Verso 2026

The manufacturer's authorised representative in the EU for product safety (GPSR) is LOGOS EUROPE, 9 rue Nicolas Poussin, 17000, La Rochelle, France
contact@logoseurope.eu

1 3 5 7 9 10 8 6 4 2

Verso
UK: 6 Meard Street, London W1F 0EG
US: 207 32nd Street, New York, NY 10016
versobooks.com

Verso is the imprint of New Left Books

ISBN-13: 978-1-83674-264-7
ISBN-13: 978-1-83674-266-1 (US EBK)
ISBN-13: 978-1-83674-265-4 (UK EBK)

British Library Cataloguing in Publication Data
A catalogue record for this book is available from the British Library

Library of Congress Cataloging-in-Publication Data

Names: Tapponi, Róisín, 1999– author
Title: Scene city : a novel / by Róisín Tapponi.
Description: New York : Verso, 2026.
Identifiers: LCCN 2026018883 (print) | LCCN 2026018884 (ebook) | ISBN 9781836742647 paperback | ISBN 9781836742661 ebk
Subjects: LCGFT: Novels
Classification: LCC PR6120.A476 S24 2026 (print) | LCC PR6120.A476 (ebook)
LC record available at https://lccn.loc.gov/2026018883
LC ebook record available at https://lccn.loc.gov/2026018884

Typeset in Electra LT by Hewer Text UK Ltd, Edinburgh
Printed and bound by CPI Group (UK) Ltd, Croydon, CR0 4YY

Scene City

A NOVEL

Róisín Tapponi

Dedicated to the memory of my grandfather Philip Coogan, whose final manuscript remained unfinished. This interruption was not on account of his death, but because his novel was about a horse breaking its ankles and, as my uncle informed him, horses don't have ankles.

Ladies and gents, you are here assembled
To hear why earth and heaven trembled
Because of the black and sinister arts
Of an Irish writer in foreign parts.

'Gas from a Burner', James Joyce

Since this is my book, and since the advent of James Joyce, why don't we let me have my way?

Eve's Hollywood, Eve Babitz

1

I cycled here and my cunt was out. Thus spoke Samira, as she pulled down her tiny dress and clip-clopped over to Closing Sale, a trendy gallery run by an art-world celesbian. The gallerist vaped and squeezed my upper arm. Have you been working out? We were joined by Teddy who had just opened his own gallery in a former fishmonger's in Bloomsbury. He tossed his hairy hands with a luxury of gestures, drawing attention to his engagement ring, worn on the wrong finger for the night. He flirted shamelessly with a conceptual artist from out of town, who cast himself as the Asian tourist in my novel. Keshav arrived, an art market consultant and *homme fatal*, the art-world version of Becky with the good hair. Disclaimer: the art world is merely a façade permitting gay men to fuck. Tom entered, a sales assistant at a Premier League–level gallery, wearing dark shades and Martine Rose football shoes that aren't even out yet. He was followed by Oscar, an emerging artist who breezed through the scene and went by the name Pope Popper. Keshav, Tom, and Oscar walked into the gallery like the first line of a pub joke, if pubs had white walls and free booze. The group chat had gathered for the opening of a group show, which was basically just an excuse for a party. The event attracted a parish of East London gays and soft-cheeked girls chewing plant-based gum wrapped up in a five-pound note. Mainly art students of the Central Saint Martins variety, and a few refined older men in suits. Do you think they're here to pick up an artwork or an art student? Samira whispered. And the rest is art history.

Main characters present and roughly established, we bagged some G&T tinnies from a small Tesco and hopped on a bus to 103 Bethnal Green Road, otherwise known as 'The Shop', infamously occupied by Tracey Emin and Sarah Lucas during their Whoreditch party girl era. Samira pointed to me, swaying on the bus. Romy kind of looks like Damien Hirst because of all the partying. If you close your eyes, we look alike. The commercial art world is so incestuous that people tend to morph into each other. See, those chromogenic prints of Richard Prince dressed as Cindy Sherman or Cindy Sherman dressed as Richard Prince. The Shop is next door to a sugaring salon which offers the best Hollywood treatment in town. The original blue exterior of the building has peeled and faded to purple. A nonsensical essay about gentrification in Shoreditch, which was surely written by a gentrifier, has been stuck to the window. It ends with the phrase: Make a difference! We're not tackling COLOUR, we're tackling humanity! BE A GIVEFUCKSTER, NOT A TRENDYHIPSTER!

The purple door was opened by a young hippie in Birkenstocks, floppy hair streaked across his forehead like wet paint. His identity was bohemian, a less authentic kind than Rainer Maria Rilke's. He introduced himself as Bartholomew. Bartholomew looked like a boy who went to boarding school and then decided to rebel by 'squatting' his £1.5 million family home. He told me his story: his father bought the building in 1999 and ousted the artists and their paraphernalia, including the titty photographs of Page Three models plastered on the basement walls. (Interjection: Page Three represents a bygone golden era in British culture and it's about time the BBC gave us a Bette Davis–inspired drama, *Whatever Happened to Katie Price?* Other key British pop culture moments: Diane Abbot publicly apologising for drinking a canned M&S mojito on the train, Phillip Schofield vaping a Lost Mary during his public TV apology, and David Hockney wearing yellow Crocs to meet the royal family.) Bartholomew said the building would soon be for sale, which was a cosmic sign. It fell on me to buy it but after rummaging in my bag all that could be offered was Fenty Beauty lip gloss. Tom told Bartholomew that it was all going to waste on him, but this authorial voice is hot so he took it gracefully. Goodbye, Bartholomew. We joined the queue for a salmon and cream cheese bagel across the road. Samira works in the publicity department of an art advisory firm and hates it. She spotted one of her colleagues inside and hid behind Tom, an effective human shield, too tall for his trousers, which he was trying to pass off as culottes.

Brick Lane was thronged with basic bitches in Adidas Samba trainers who descend on the weekend to photograph the hipster graffiti and visit the tacky vintage shops. Something about vintage clothing never sat right with me. Growing up, you didn't want to be caught wearing someone else's hand-me-downs. The best vintage shops in the area are Aro Archive and West Archive, otherwise you'd be better off heading to Notting Hill for more esoteric thirdhand vintage. Recently we were all at a party in Notting Hill, and Teddy scoffed at a teenage boy cosplaying as a 1950s heart-throb. He swaggered around in a pastel vintage suit with a lock of hair gelled to his forehead and a toothpick hanging from his lips. Oscar agreed that he looked ridiculous. Tom said he was probably something to do with the indie sleaze revival. Keshav suggested that he was undergoing past-life regression therapy. Samira choked on her canapé. Bless him, she said, it's just one of the Beckham children. We floated down Brick Lane alongside flumes of fried grease, punctuating our walk at the Golden Heart, an iconic local pub once frequented by the YBAs. We walked up to the bar, where tequila was slopped into shot glasses and heads shot back. A full shot is like a full stop, it only takes one to start a new chapter. And luckily, this was a night when everybody seemed to be expecting something. Bought a few bags of scampi crisps, which are currently experiencing a revival. The walls were plastered with YBA prints, one of the many reasons why the drinks were so bloody expensive.

My phone vibrated with a text from Florine, the princess of Liechtenstein, who is soon going to open her own gallery.

She was still hungover from the Richard Prince dinner last night at Cipriani. That is the virtue of anaesthetics. Paul drunkenly snuck up behind me, a pint of plain in each hand. Many details of our research trip hereafter are unpublishable because Paul said this document of felonious narcotism would jeopardise his very serious editor-in-chief position at a seriously serious magazine. Herein, certain substances are substituted with the words *Percy Pigs*. Paul was on a date in the other room with a *Death in Venice*–type boy who works at the French deli on Broadway Market. Paul was out looking for a hole but all he found was wholesome. The boy's bedtime came around soon enough so Paul joined our table and we did more rounds of shots, until it became increasingly unlikely that we would be able to convince any other venue to let us in. This was probably for the best, as by this point even the table had begun dribbling. Teddy and Tom disappeared into the little Beuy's room and came back with a screenplay.

TEDDY, 30, and TOM, 30, wait in the queue for the men's bathroom. MAN, 30s, stands behind them. MAN is from Barnet and works as General Manager of M&S Finsbury Park.

MAN

Do you want to help me in the bathroom?

TEDDY AND TOM

(prepared to have a threesome)

Yes.

MAN whips out Percy Pigs and Prius car keys.

TEDDY AND TOM

Are you not going to take your dick out?

MAN

No, I'm not, but I thought we could do some—

TEDDY

Not with Prius car keys . . .

Pinter pause.

MAN

I did once fuck a man at uni.

MAN panics and leaves. He runs back to kiss TEDDY on the forehead.

MAN (CONT'D)

Beautiful man.

TEDDY

My marriage is over.

Tom should dress up as cocaine on Halloween so someone would do him in the bathroom. The women's bathroom was occupied by Keshav who harvested a bag of Percy Pigs in his bulging pants. He rambled on about a book called *Cruising Materialisms*, blah-blah queer futurity blah-blah. Go piss, girl. Putto, the chubby cherubs from Fiorucci t-shirts, covered the toilet cubicle ceiling. In my drunken stupor their mournful expressions illuminated the difference between paint and pain. We joined Paul outside and Keshav rambled about Swiss Bank blah-blah Silicon Valley Bank collapse blah-blah. Notes of a cigarette tickled his nostrils and its smoke formed grey strings in the sky as the evening played an air. Is the sky trash? The sky is a dustbin for grey clouds. Paul had enough of our nonsense and went back inside. Keshav told everyone that Paul only left because he fancied him, but Keshav thinks everyone fancies him.

All of us are enchanted by the brooding emotions that Paul derives from his solitude, which is somehow less depressing than the numbness felt by many others in the art world. Oscar wanted curry chips, but the kitchen was closed. Samira straddled the jukebox and tried to change the music because someone had queued the Smiths. HOW MANY GAYS DOES IT TAKE TO WORK A JUKE BOX? she yelled. Teddy clapped along to the Smiths and had a great time. The disposable camera, purchased earlier at Eye Culture on Bethnal Green Road, was not in Oscar's handbag as it should have been. However, there was an EpiPen and some poppers which, funnily enough, bore the name Bartholomew, like the heir to the Shop. Bad day to be called Bartholomew. Put but poppers in thy purse. Teddy had the camera and was flashing all over the place.

I'm not embarrassed about the photos.
All I want is to be famous. Like the YBAs.
Teddy

Paul ran away and later told us he had gotten into a car crash. We would have killed him if he'd died. Keshav flaunted his nice arms and reminded everyone that he runs each morning. From whom? Tom convinced Helen, the proprietor, to take a photo with us. She was only being nice because Tom told her we all worked at the Tate. Helen had more powder on her face than a bag of Percy Pigs, doubly paled by her ghostly life of art-world lore and its shrivelled cocaine hearts. The Golden Heart closed so we drunkenly careened to the Queen Adelaide, a queer pub reincarnated by the former owners of the George and Dragon. Oscar did his first group exhibition there, viz a project called the White Cubicle. We found an empty room and danced in a trance for two hours to French rap. The bars have lowered, young rappers are spitting captions. Everyone exercised their limbs and jaws with more and more Percy Pigs. Teddy got bored of the music and began swinging his hips, singing Madonna's 'Papa Don't Preach', replacing papa with popper. We could have danced forever and we all moved in slow motion like we were in a film. Oscar bought five packs of KP nuts and ate them all. He and Keshav made out for the seventh time this year. They disappeared at some point, and the rest of us eventually staggered outside, dazed.

We headed over to a seedy strip club opposite Bethnal Green station. Each Friday night it transforms into a queer strip club, where the girls want to be the dancers, not just be with them. However, this was a straight night. Nina Simone's 'Sinnerman' echoed from scratchy speakers and a pound coin lay sadly beneath the stripper pole, which is how you know there's an upcoming recession. Tom flopped down in the front row and looked like he was waiting to be called at the GP's. He recognised one of the strippers, a cultural strategist concerned with political change beyond representation. She had recently delivered an online lecture about how the essence of DEI is inclusion in white spaces, so why should Black and brown people care? It wasn't long until we were kicked out because Tom had too many Percy Pigs and OD'd at the strip club. Masticated girl dinner puked from his mouth like Pallas Athena from the head of Zeus. We ordered him a cab, remembering his new home address. Romy remembers everything, Teddy said, eyeing me suspiciously. Samira sped past in her tiny dress on a Lime bike and screamed goodnight to anyone who would listen. The bus was slow to arrive. It was difficult to pick out the droplets dampening my skin. The ground was muddied with footfall, under clouds swollen with rain. The night drained the street of colour and yawned into day. The gorgeous orange rag of a sunrise was hung to dry across the wet sky.

2

Samira is doing freelance publicity for Wayne King, an underground filmmaker specialising in gay pornography. The poster for his upcoming film depicts Big Ben ejaculating. Samira teased it out of her bag at Café Helen, wafting it in greasy air, telling us about it between mouthfuls of her second shawarma wrap. See shawarma meat on the stake like Joan of Arc. Keshav decided to audition for the film. He would be able to get by solely on his looks, in case things went tits up in his journalism career. The next day, King took one look at Keshav and cast him on the spot. However, he was cast as a straight man. Keshav literally had to walk into a scene in his little Paloma Wool pullover and suck a tit on camera. Like Stephen Dedalus, he was almosting it. Once before, Keshav performed heterosexuality, at the Serpentine Summer Party. His eyes fluttered their wings at a socialite, who had inherited a country house and a prescription drug problem. He only did it because he wanted to get with her sexy boyfriend, who used to work at a gallery, and had upgraded from assistant to client. They ended up having a threesome, except the boyfriend just sat and watched, meaning that Keshav basically just fucked a woman, licking her vagina lips like an envelope. Anyway, Keshav wanted us all to come support his porn debut, and that's how we found ourselves at a porn shoot on Eid.

What's Eid? Teddy asked me as we jogged down the escalator in Old Street station. It's Christmas for Muslims. It was the day of a big football match, so the train carriage was engulfed by lads in scarves who beat the air oddly. One of them carefully placed dried snot scooped from his right nostril on the moquette of the Tube seat. It was also rush hour, so everyone stood very straight like the figures in Rothko's early *Subway* paintings, sucking their breath and holding their stomachs in to create more space in the stinking carriage. Rocking in the cot of an unventilated Northern Line, it felt like we were inside a cocktail shaker. Gasping for air, we re-emerged in Bermondsey, the new residential trap for young white middle-class families. Being residential in the city means knowing when is bin day. We took a pit-stop at a speciality coffee shop. A gentle skimmer, the pale and tattooed barista poured pea milk into my flat white. Teddy flirted with him between deep drags on his watermelon-flavoured vape, inhaling nicotine down to his toes. Life goes fast, one minute you're sucking a dummy and the next minute it's a vape. We admired the barista's revolutionary biceps and the prosperous bulge of his grey joggers. The man was Apollonian. His throat held the golden apple of the sun. Teddy sank two lumps of sugar deftly longwise into a batch brew, as if it was an art and this was our culture.

The porn shoot took place in someone's bachelor pad, decorated with garish fluorescent bulbs and stocked with cheap wine. The floor was covered with linoleum as dubiously grimy as the women's bathrooms in the Spurstowe Arms, a neighbourhood pub where you're guaranteed to bump into someone you don't want to know. Once in the bathrooms there was a throng of Northern Irish girls shooting up what appeared to be drugs but on closer inspection was actually Botox. Keshav once kissed Botox lips. He said they were surprisingly hard, rather than pillowy soft. The odour of Lynx Africa polluted the bachelor pad; it was not long before sex broke out. To watch you had to bend over and ogle through anus-sized peepholes. My body was wound tight as a violin string, still vibrating from last night. The first sex acts were brief because the woman cringed at most of the things the men tried to do to make it last longer. Her painted red lips were a gaping hole that swallowed almost anything. A man foraged in the belly of the woman with his sausage roll. Stalled in missionary position, her knees sprung outwards like an umbrella. His flesh covered her completely. Everyone's sex organs were soggy with rendezvous. The kitchen contained men who fucked like gastropods and left trails of slime on the tiles. A noose for choking hung crudely like a Tampax string. The living room hosted a queerly Catholic gathering of genuflecting bottoms, cupped like chalices. An armada of bottoms. In the corner of the backstage area, an extra wearing an ungirdled yellow dressing gown lay asleep in a rocking chair, modestly concealed by Natasha Lyonne's face on the cover of the *Evening Standard*. The man's weather-beaten visage remained motionless, but his fist clamped a bottle of wine. Passion falls asleep.

My elliptical encrustations darted around the room, drunkenly searching for phrases. The experience was entirely literary. Samuel Beckett wrote *Murphy* in a notebook he nicknamed whoroscope. Seeing with eyes like roving hands, my gaze was answered by a bear cosplaying as an estate agent, who motioned me over with the determined pudginess of small fists. The man wore a plaid shirt, chinos, and an aggressive amount of hair gel, which gave his military shave the air of dew on wet grass. He was in the closet for so long that you think he'd have found some decent clothes. The meridian of our interests was Salma Hayek. We discussed her recent performance in the feel-bad film *Magic Mike's Last Dance*. It was set in London without having anything recognisably London about it, aside from the interior of a theatre which looked like the one in Ken Russell's *The Boy Friend*, starring Twiggy with her hackneyed accent. Our discussion extended to other actors like Renée Zellweger, who's the most British non-British person ever. Why are you doing a PhD in art history when you're obsessed with films? he asked me. We're in the era of the screen. And my thesis is called *The Dialectical Aesthetics of Video Art in Palestine since the 1970s*. Right. The bear identified as LGBTQIA2S+. Premium gay without the ads. He discovered he wasn't straight because he actually liked women. His husband made trendy airbrush paintings. He had a flat with air-conditioning and a morphine addiction. Morphine makes everything seem important, a line spoken by a sick man at the beginning of Michelangelo Antonioni's *La Notte*. The bear solemnly bowed his head, a gesture that would have been graceful had he been someone else.

This porn shoot is *not* a chic experience, Teddy moaned, scratching his beard. We had envisioned a backstage similar to the mise-en-scène of back-shots in Andy Warhol's pornographic film theatre, *Boys to Adore Galore*, or the glamorously theatrical porn set in Brian De Palma's *Body Double*. The film being shot right now did at least feature elderly women who looked fabulously camp. They wore cheap wigs that slid off their heads as they moved up and down, mingling pudgy fingers and buttery glances in some sausage and mash sex. The lead actor was sexy: he did not have mere thighs but thighs celestial. Thighs as thick as a horse's belly, with a variegated naevus on the surface of the right arse cheek that held Tom spellbound. Fucking him would be like having the Uffizi all to yourself. We spied Keshav naked in the corner, rotating a knot out of his shoulder, and lecturing a mattress actress about Swiss Bank. The lead actor undid his tie and inserted his dry leather tongue into another mouth. Everything was up in the air and under the merciless overhead lighting. Licked my lips. Drink some water, Tom muttered. I am. That's coffee. It's got water in it. Everyone spoke in the hushed whisper of a prayer whilst the actors exerted their limbs and whistled through their teeth like boiling kettles. To quote Diderot's *Jacques the Fatalist* with noetic ascent, he found himself underneath her and consequently she found herself on top of him. Stop quoting people, Teddy hissed. Not him being bossy, in his bossy era.

The silicone fuckable foot was explored by Oscar and a man with a Kaws tattoo on his chest. He was a bodybuilder and his head bounced like a nodding dog on a dashboard. He downed a Magnum tonic wine in one gulp. Since Oscar was otherwise engaged, an elderly costume stylist broached a conversation. Where are you from? she asked. Tapped my head. She looked like a frumpy librarian with a wispy pony-tail, as if she had rubbed her head against a balloon. Told her about the giant scrunchie phenomenon. Networking in the porn industry involves less rizz than in the film industry. The woman yapped and my gaze fixed itself on the pale blue blush of her eyes. In each room were two large flatscreen TVs. The first projected the live porn action and the second was showing *Loose Women*. The director screamed shrilly for the stylist. Two sets of twins reclined on grubby cushions and made love, him on his and his on him. His callipygian asset was tight as the buttonhole of a shirt. The Saviour bumped upon a heavy butt, once wrote Rimbaud. Everyone fucked until they forgot the sad things that have happened. My body stood motionless as the sex continued, feeling the afternoon run through its zodiac. It was raining bricks which hit the window in a non-stop round of applause whilst moans poured down with growing intensity. Teddy was vaping outside. The rain fell onto his balding scalp and plopped onto the pavement like blood clots. Teased the moon from my belly button and a period flowed.

The rain spat and the sky rumbled in disapproval at all that was taking place below.

Teddy and Tom tried to make me eat locally at some misoteric Japanese restaurant, but that wasn't going to happen, not in Bermondsey. We walked past a buzzy new small-plates establishment, but they had hummus on the menu. Samira consulted Google. Nope. Lamb chops at Tayyabs? Nope, Teddy won't eat spicy. Quality Chop House? Too expensive. So we returned to Shoreditch, seeking the familiar landscape of cranes cutting the air and steel arms pushing away the sky. The grey clouds continued to accumulate and looked like nubbins of dust from a vacuum cleaner. London is an ontology of greyness and the architecture of its sky is mapped in construction cranes. My favourite building in Shoreditch is the car wash on Great Eastern Street. It is verifiably dodgy and definitely a money-laundering front. When we grow rich, say the bells of Shoreditch. While passing the hurdy-gurdy washing machine of the car wash my imagination conjures the nefarious activities taking place inside. There were a few Reddit sub-threads about the car wash, but all the pages have been mysteriously deleted. Around this corrupt relic, office spaces have begun to spread like a virus.

Our haunted houses are futuristic: skeletons of new buildings on sites which kill construction workers. These global mausoleums are built for art, we visit them and say: Wow. Isn't it beautiful? The new glass residential buildings in Shoreditch are identical to the office buildings, except people live in them. Everything is all the same, said Teddy.

Everyone has nipples. Samira joined us and reminded us to eat. My stomach rumbled and interrupted my voluptuous thoughts. Girl lunch usually consists of bone broth and a handful of Medjool dates. We went to an upstairs modern British restaurant on Redchurch Street and dined on farls of sourdough sodden with butter, sun-bronzed grains and strong-smoked sole. Ate up Houellebecq's rollmop herrings of choucroute royale. Proust's madeleines, Foster Wallace's Toblerones. There was a couple sat at the table next to us on a date. She talked about astrology, while he squirmed against the pressure of the hurling stick in his jeans. They were soon joined by a knucklehead who once sexted Samira in the bleak midwinter. He was a ratty mid-tier gallerist who stole artists once smaller galleries had built up their markets. Samira looked upset. So did Teddy. He had forgotten the name of his childhood hamster. Democritus Junior, to the reader. They did a line. How are you going to fall in love when you can't even fall asleep? Piss off, Romy.

Following dinner, we enjoyed a quiet night at Penetration Palace. It's a longish-running heavy-techno and sweat-heavy club night at a pub in Homerton. The place was full of club kids. They wore dew-blanched horns and shook the plums of their arses within the aural glen. They trampled forth to chant the Azealia Banks songs that roused them of old, footing it all night on manky disco tiles. Loosened a tress of the starry eddies of my ponytail. We used to go to PDA (RIP), Anal House Meltdown and Pussy Palace club nights, which probably still exist, with a younger crowd of bodies bending to a baseline below the waistline. Video art used to be shown in the club. Lawrence Weiner, Dara Birnbaum, and Tony Oursler were projected in video lounges at the Mudd Club, Danceteria, and Palladium. Now, the medium has migrated to the walls of white cubes for the enjoyment of sex pests who practise stealth wealth.

Our medium is the city. Grinding on Grindr, every party we attend is a gay party, which is why Samira believes she is single. She had tried looking confused in London Fields Lido. Lido libido. Last week, an Israeli percussionist had the audacity to fumble her, Samira, a Muslim baddie. Samira saw a guy on Hinge called Israel. Being called Israel in the 2020s is like being called Isis in the 2010s. She asked me to instead orchestrate a date with a composer in my network. Sigh. God's plan for you does not involve experimental musicians. Too much fretwork. Besides, he is too nonchalant, you're looking for chalant. Whatever, they still hooked up, and Samira has a video of him masturbating to a metronome. Then she gave him the silent treatment and posted a thirst trap on her stories; he knew it was over. Florine arrived at the club, moonstruck by her wandering eye. She carried a bunch of flowers wrapped in green waxed paper, challenging the chemsex sweat of the bar with wafts of the clammy earth-smells of her bouquet.

Florine distributed her flowers throughout the club, leftovers from her side quest, a flower business/supper club. In *Chéri*, Colette argued that perfume works best when soaked into sagging flesh, which is something to look forward to about growing old. Florine philosophised with me on bar stools with pints of Guinness while nosey breasts pushed up against my back. Do you know how to get on the Coperni PR list? the stranger slurred into my ear. Forgot her name, but she's Californian and the epitome of succubus chic. Beside her, an up-and-coming someone introduced himself as a music video director. He asked me to recommend a silly little small-plate restaurant with esoteric cocktails. Took a machine gun from behind my back and shot them. Just kidding. Looked upwards beseechingly, the red lights of the dingy pub were the same as at the porn shoot. Men jerked in rhythm to the music and jerked off with each other. Schismatic sect, mingling hands and mingling dances. Glitter freckled my arms. Teddy smuggled more bags of Percy Pigs into the establishment and then broke my JW Anderson pigeon bag, so now he's disabled. (The pigeon, not Teddy.) Although Teddy is secretly rachitic. Ratchet? Rickety? He has rickets. In the holiest of Penetration Palace moments the boys stick their heads through crests of ecstasy which pass like a wave in a fabulous crash of blood. Feelings of love pulsed within my heart, we're so happy to be afraid tonight.

3

In the beginning was the Word document. The poor poets wake from disturbed dreams to paint an image of the morning which happened without them. Still abandoning myself and evading self-reflection. Mirroring the city, stuck in my surface stage. Female protagonists of novels are often expected to reflect upon their feelings. Here, you can extract meaning from my life lived outside. My interiority is reserved, speaking always in my own voice but keeping myself secret, a table for one. Here is a naked mind, *super spottum*. But the rest of my body is my own. Turning myself in without turning inwards, an NPC in A.P.C. People who only use their mind to think do not think enough, especially when the body is at stake. Do you believe in life after love? See, an image of the world screenshot by my eyes for you. Paul Éluard wrote a poem for Pablo Picasso, Stéphane Mallarmé scrawled a sonnet for Édouard Manet and René Char penned a verse for Gustave Courbet, translated by

Samuel Beckett. Charles Baudelaire was down bad for Eugène Delacroix. Scores of writers connected with artists through poems and so you have my words. Tired of posing for poems by men? Here, hungover thoughts served to you on a silver tray by the soles of my hands and the palms of my feet. Enough, there is more party, still. Breakfast, then awakes the world!

Breakfast winds flatulated anti-monarchy protestors who ceremoniously swarmed the road in front of the Buckingham Palace. There were even some TikTokers wearing anti-surveillance makeup, which felt very après-garde. A timely restoration of Isaac Julien's 1991 *Young Soul Rebels* was screening at the ICA cinema. The film's punk protagonists throw an anti–Silver Jubilee party in a park near Dalston. Then a fight breaks out among chants threaded together into a vocal chain. There are never physical fights like that in the art world, except for the time Tom punched Teddy, a boring bitch fest that ended with: All you think about are seating arrangements.

PREVIEWS OF COMING ATTRACTIONS. Thought it would be fun to host my own anti-monarchy party for the coronation, in commemoration of our un-united kingdom. This is an Irish book trapped in England and such activity is my birthright. The coronation is today but a united Ireland is forever, my Irish mother texted. She is more invested in *Coronation Street* than the coronation. In Easter 1916, a terrible beauty was born. The poster for my party was made while sat on the toilet and comprised a screenshot of the lyrics of 'Go on Home, British Soldiers' by the Wolfe Tones. It listed key logistical information and a dress code, which was 'favourite terrorist', according to any definition of the word. From Al Capone to Al Qaeda, Bobby Sands to Leila Ahmed, etc.

Samira was my co-host and arrived on my doorstep early in a fake Chanel outfit from Turkey. Pass me a fridge cigarette. Tossed her a Coke Zero. Took a shower. *Na'eeman.* Got dressed. Opened the drawer of my brás cubas and pulled out two letters, DD, for my full stops. Samira shouted from outside my bedroom door that she knew a terrorist from school. One day he was singing 'Baa, Baa, Black Sheep' and the next he had joined ISIS. Samira whirled across the living room with belly-dancing-style scarves tied around thick thighs that jingled with every step. We masqueraded as Western stereotypes, hardcore versions of how *they* see *us*. When did fakes gain value? Samira asked, jingling her fake Chanel sequined hip scarf. When they started printing money. Reproductions were given value; like the old fake French restaurants in midtown New York. Lutèce, Le Steak de Paris, La Côte Basque, La Grenouille, La Caravelle. Frog Pond, as Tom Wolfe put it. Samira drained her Coke and listened to my shouting over a Dyson Supersonic Diffuser. Nothing stands between production and consumption anymore. When there's nothing left of ourselves to exploit, you know what'll happen? We'll cannibalise ourselves. Jesus, Romy. No, it's true. Metaphorically, at least. Well, I'd rather have someone else eat me out than have to eat myself. Come on then, let's find you a cannibal.

We paraded up Shoreditch High Street in anti-monarchical regalia to a neighbourhood pub which smelt like stale piss, nestled within a nearby Hoxton estate. My favourite smell is the turf burning in the hearth of my grandparents' bungalow in occupied Ireland. The front door, never used. Someone should make a turf perfume, the cottagecore girlies would eat it up. The main thing my city apartment and my grandma's home have in common are the raffle tickets littered everywhere. Hers are from church bingo, mine from nightclub cloakrooms. Shepherd's pie and scratch cards and crosswords and Danielle Steel softcovers and almanac hardbacks and Christmas cards hung on string across the wall, to the soundtrack of the *Heartbeat* title song. Horse betting on Istabraq. Vintage photographs of the ford of Snámh Dá Éan. My grandfather was an author, to whom this book is dedicated. He was also a reiki master. My family are so Irish that Yorkshire puddings have been banned from the Christmas dinner. Will you have a Baileys or Sheridan's? Go on, you will, you will.

Friends had already arrived with their friends, including an American art collector who sat at the bar looking for something stiff and a drink. He's known for writing off millions of dollars in federal taxes by donating artworks to museums. The skin on his face peeled from a sunburn, a self-imposed exile in Mustique where he found the gesso within. He looked like a slice of crusty week-old sourdough. Paul left no crumbs. They soon left together and Paul told me the next day he was going to join the Baader-Meinhof Group. Keshav won best-dressed, donning an outfit inspired by the CCTV image of Kim Jong-nam's suspected assassin at an airport, wearing a t-shirt reading LOL. He had crossed out I TOLD YA on his Loewe t-shirt and scrawled LOL. He wore a wig. The assassin looked like a femme fatale; she had the same sleek black bob as the manic pixie dream girls in Hal Hartley's *Amateur*, Luc Besson's *Léon* and Tarantino's *Pulp Fiction*. These films were all, coincidentally, shot in 1994. Then Teddy arrived. Oi, you lot. Where's Oscar? He's coffined in a cab with his LA dealer. Drugs or art? Not sure. He soon pulled up. It's not a drug habit, he insisted, just a nasal habit. Tom arrived with company. Meet my new two-legged friend, he said. He entered with a cute girl who later got acne and tried to kill herself under the starry pimples of the night. She wrote herself a prescription, and her ex-boyfriend's name was mentioned on it. Why are they friends? Keshav asked. Because he's a gay man and she's a fag hag? No. Because he's fat and she's skinny? Stop. Who is she? Samira whispered. She's *on the verge*. Of what? Being famous. For what? No-one knows. The girl pulled out big sunglasses. She actually kept them in their case. What are you, a serial killer? Teddy asked.

Physical descriptions of the most regular partygoers have been omitted. This is because readers often enjoy imagining such things for themselves. It's like playing *The Sims* or *Stardoll*, where you can create your own avatars. In a similar vein, most people enjoy casting the hero or romantic protagonist according to their own preferences. Unfortunately, there's nothing much heroic or romantic about any of the characters here. But in the privacy of your imagination – this is when it gets interesting! – you may represent your prejudices at pleasure. Like an Arab child in

The Recognitions, running around dirty and selling peanuts and hashish from a basket. Since I'm half-Arab — there you go — you may feel a trace of 9/11 terror and so be inclined to imagine Saddam Hussein with tits. Usually, people like me are only allowed to write books about war. Or if we write about anything else, our identity can't come into it. Because then, why aren't we writing about war? Conservative book publishers want me to be a mouthpiece for conflict, they don't want me to have fun. Publish and be damned. Even if you can't identify with me at all, please keep reading. These days, people expect to see themselves in everything. And if they don't, it's a problem. But you're all welcome here. (No RSVP necessary.)

Nearby, a swarthy man opened a punk zine and propped it nimbly upon his Japanese messenger bag, a former viceroy of Vice Media who dressed as himself. He wore a *Friday* film poster t-shirt and vehemently criticised the racial politics of a new exhibition by a Black artist, and then admitted that he hadn't seen the show. Mentioned that my boyfriend, Caleb, has been discussing with me the prospect of moving to a more residential area where we'd know our neighbours, somewhere with more green space. So a posh neighbourhood? *Friday* asked with a smug smile. Nodded. Tom later chastised me in the smoking area, flourishing his smoking arm, for not cussing out *Friday*. You're a fool, Romy, a fool in a foulard. Keshav joined us. David Foster Wallace wore a bandana so Romy could wear a Hermès foulard. Smacked them both. Tom took out a used butt and lit up. *Friday* brought a corny girl, underfed and bleached, who kept using the phrase Peckham supremacy. She spoke pointedly, as if her speech had speech marks. 'You know what they say,' she said jauntily, 'New Delhi, New York, New Cross.' Tom's eyes rolled. People from the most affluent backgrounds are those most critical of anyone else who wants something nice. How do we make them go away? Refresh. A teen in a shiesty masqueraded as the viral Tabi thief. He was Teddy's friend, a suburban rapper, who'd gone from Postman Pat to Project Pat. His body was gangly like a grass stem and his buzz cut was fastidiously mown. He looked like a skater, but couldn't skate. Then again, most of Teddy's friends do not skateboard, they charcuterie board.

Tired of ourselves, we had become other people. In the smoking area, Osama bin Laden snogged Maximilien Robespierre. Cigarette ash rested on his hair like snow. Chairman Mao tossed Benito Mussolini in the bathroom. The long labours of the toilet ceased. Mussolini fastened his jeans as he exited the bathroom, and his zipper snarled. There were fake tan stains on the toilet bowls. Maud Gonne beat everyone at pool, a Fenian dressed in Willy Chavarria. If she hadn't repeatedly rejected the advances of W. B. Yeats, we wouldn't have our poetry. She was averse to versifiers. Romantic Ireland's dead and gone, it's with W. B. Yeats in the grave. O, the witty epitaphs of tombstones or Instagram captions. An elderly woman sat at the bar with her dog Argus. She herself was named Barbara and used to be in a punk band. Barbara and the Barbarities. She was not a member of our party but nonetheless engaged Benjamin Netanyahu in a conversation about Yorkshire terrorists.

He looked exceptionally fictional, wearing a codpiece and Sinéad O'Dwyer Shibari leggings.

Someone entered the bar who once occupied Oscar's dreams, and then his nightmares. Oscar was in one of my dreams a few nights ago. In the dream, his forehead creases were vertical. My living nightmare landed in my inbox the next morning: an invitation to a Soho House brunch hosted by a feminist art historian influencer. Barf. The fact that she even invited me made me want to kill myself. She's the next Winona Ryder, Tom whispered, pointing to a girl at the bar. Who was the last Winona Ryder? There wasn't any music, so someone took off their clothes and played themselves. I'm not a trans artist, I'm a gender illusionist, they moaned tautologically into a broken microphone. The Irish barman refused to serve a Guinness to Oliver Cromwell, who had elbowed in front of Teddy. *Up the RA*, the barman winked at us. The Royal Academy? Jesus Christ, Teddy. Christopher Columbus was barred re-entry because the bouncer mistook his crossed eyes for symptoms of extreme drunkenness. He complained about the lack of straight and single women at the party. There is probably a woman in a flowing skirt with an Aperol spritz singing 'Video Games' at karaoke in Dalston as we speak, we told him, waiting for you. Off he went. *Anseo*, meaning here, here and now, all present and correct, stuck in the horror of the endlessly refreshing now.

Slip the thready stems of daisies, delay the drunken dawn, and smooth the papery legacies of beer mats. Fleshy lips began forming thick sentences as tipsy terrorists slammed beer glasses, straddled ripped upholstered stools, and knocked heads against swinging light bulbs. Thong out, string of a violin played by men in a thronged bar. There was no mercy for any of us whose crucifix of lisle legs crossed underneath stained wooden tables. More friends with friends arrived until our terrorist group occupied the whole pub and spilled onto the street. The past, present, and future walked into the bar, it was tense. Ha. The bartender soon rang the bell for last orders and we sloshed out of the pub into the night, lit brightly by pollution. London's night sky becomes easily stuck in twilight and smog to blur the scarred moon. In a stupor, staring at a night sky yellowed by smoke. Tom suggested that we host the after-party at his new place. He wanted us all to see it. After scores of sleepless nights on Zoopla, he had found his fantasy: somewhere affordable to live alone. He grabbed his phone to show us pictures. His lock screen was a photo of a woman. Isn't that your therapist? The rest of the night was wiped from my memory with face cleanser. Literature only gives us two options: to live or to recount. When you are living, little happens. The set changes, people come in and out and that's it. Days become one long party without chapters to break them. Then comes the final full stop. Such an uninteresting way to mark an ending.

The only comment made in my Notes app was *the elegance of stumpy trees* which presumably referred to the bare-knuckled trees of Hoxton. Have recently began taking notes on nights out. It helps me remember in the morning. Wait, there was an owl trying to tell me something. The midnight pavement spun itself from our feet. We weeded through an allotment. A terrorist played pop songs recalling the things that most people desire, while a cigarette dangled from his mouthpiece. The girlies looked like dryads, and the branches sketched bark against the bricks of buildings. In *Episodes of the Cuban Revolutionary War*, Che Guevara referenced a novel about a hero who leaned against a tree. The heavy boughs, their sigh of falling leaves, each leaf became a red flag in the wind. The Guevara quote introduced *Meeting*, a short story by Julio Cortázar about a tree. Keshav took a detour and hooked up with a guy on Grindr, also underneath a tree. Grindr leaves nothing to fate anymore. Keshav with moon-blanched skin plucked a date with wrinkled flesh tawny from a keto diet. He dropped to more applause than a Phoebe Philo drop. His body then climbed atop the stranger's tree trunk and the act gave him splinters, two bare shells in the moonshine. Who are you? Someone to whom things happen. And where did you learn to give head like that? A museum's disabled bathroom. Moon, you celestial onion.

At Tom's new house, the coronation was celebrated with a recreation of Rob Pruitt's infamous artwork *Cocaine Buffet* exhibited in 1998 at the Fifth International, a distant art world memory of Old York. 'Twas on a Holy Thursday, or something. The girls emptied baggies of Percy Pigs down the length of the living room. My drooping eyes bore witness to the end of their ancestral lines. Everyone proceeded to act pussified and dramatic. May all ups and downs remain under the sheets. Samira lay in the crook of Tom's armpit on his bed, a timber article of advanced age. She looked beautiful, her face was wrapped with hair, and a Le Creuset crúiskeen was balanced on the hillock of her knees. She was fit spoil for a centaur, with such shapely knees. Someone visited her mouth for a cinematic snog. She lowered her false eyelashes and drifted from consciousness. My fingernails picked buttercups off the quilt. Everyone misplaced words like pebbles in strange formations of sentences, which were exchanged in dark corners of the kitchen, bedroom and bathroom, comma chameleons, punctuated by occasional disappearances into Bethnal Green Gardens. Pulled the window to my eyes and looked beyond the pane. Lips blow a flute alive, a gay open-air performance. He took his meat out. Wind whips the flame. How would you like me? Medium rare. His and his mouths neared. His lipped his. Ta langue, touch 'em well. Caecum digested cum, whilst Lime bikes rested against lime trees.

Found the aux cord and played *Gay Guerrilla*. Julius Eastman's piano score cut through whispers with crisp delirium. Secrets were softly spoken, a diaspora of erotic exchanges and misplaced insecurities exiled to more welcoming ears. The molly mollified Molly, who lay on the floor with a cigarette sighing apostrophically from her mouth. Molly is not the soul of a city laid bare, she is what happens when a soul leaves the body. Pupils blinked staccato with the rise of music to mezcal shots and the fall of feet that made intimate contact with the wooden floor. Sup and bowse from horn and can. Everyone danced, tarry buccaneers with hands of bacca quids and rings ringing in their ears. Movement was disguised as rhythm under the dim lights, and bodies swayed sleepily to a sweet dream. Someone's sonshine vomited. Burning cheeks with a gaze. Lovers alone, lovers protect. Limbs leaned lightly on other limbs and the languid lovers loosened their belts with tongues. Swans of songs surrounded cygnets in signet rings and other baroque effigies of gilded dalliance. It was an easily romantic affair, a party where so many hearts chose to share. Escorted by stars, dressed as the flowers of the sky, the sun soon chewed the moon.

4

Birdsong of bin lorries broke my sleep. Defined by a hangover, the morning allowed no daybreak thesis editing for one soon to be a doctor, joining the ranks of Dr Umar and Dr Barbara Sturm. Chucked a pillow across the room, waited to see if something would happen. When it did not, my legs swung my feet out of bed. My teeth practically brushed themselves. Looked in my front camera, despite the bathroom mirror in front of me. Applied lipstick, upon reflection. These hungover days are awful because they dim the clarity required for the mind to form neat sentences within a specific scholarly format. My natural sentences are cluttered and overgrown, having grown up without the aesthetic value of minimalism and quiet luxury, where everything is hidden. Each morning has become a morning after, and every night there is an event. The necessity of it has all come into question, catechised by an Irish mind which has sinned. The Irish desire? To one day see a puffin. Lessened my guilt and thought about it this way: partying is resistance against a society where everything must lead to financial gain. The art world is super into resistance right now. Everything is supposedly resistance, but the rise of far-right governance is not resisted. Continue partying, but stop before it becomes wretched.

Someone critically renowned once advised me that it is better to write while hungover, because fewer famous authors have done it. The most canonical men have already written everything there is to say whilst blind drunk, he said. If you want to artistically compete with Fitzgerald or Hemingway, then you would have to out-drink them. That is not possible for you, my dear, because your weight must not exceed 55kg if you want to remain on all the guest lists. The man must have been right, since he now has a Pulitzer Prize and a drinking problem. He also said that living 'the art life' and having a PhD won't make the adults take me seriously. What is taken seriously? Money. Well, how does one come across that? It's too late, my dear, you've read too much. These financiers are already too far ahead. Some blue shirts walked past us. Well, how are *those* guys taken seriously.What is taken seriously? Money. Well, how does one come across that? It's too late, my dear, you've read too much. Some blue shirts walked past us. Well, how are those losers taken seriously I know, I know, he sighed. It's depressing.

My hand sat down to write bony letters with a cheap ballpoint pen of malnourished ink, and my drowsy hair spilled over the back of my chair. There is a thigh gap between most industries and their scholars. Despite my studies towards a PhD in art history, my feelings of being an art historical fraud remain. There is a historical distance between academia and the art world. The YBAs mostly studied at Goldsmiths, but one of their cohort went to the Slade. A stalwart of the scene, she partied with them every night. Some of the YBAs visited the Slade to deliver a guest lecture, with much feet-kissing by the professors, who were confused and impressed by how one of their students obviously knew them too intimately. It doesn't matter, anyhow. My favourite kind of art history is gossip over fried chicken and pisco sours at Claridge's, exchanging tattle which will become scholarship decades later. Our footsteps will become footnotes. History is delulu, this century exposing the lies of last century. It's all fiction anyway and, in a city of no morals, lying means having a gift for fiction. We're fictionalying. We're stuck and will discover the consequences in the second half of the century. TBC.

There are many art histories of the city. Each area of London breeds multiple ways of living and specific social codes. The more anthropological knowledge you accumulate about your scene, the more club-card loyalty points you acquire, and that's how you slowly become accustomed to the system. That's how it works, for those of us not already born into a subdivision of the 'global elite' with the knowledge of how to navigate it. Maybe my code-switching will become so seamless one day that this silly narrator will begin to fool themselves. But I'm not going to treat you like a fool, reader. You get enough of that from the government. Always better to keep one ballet flat in and out of it all, with elegant woes bending to the sublime, prancing around London. There is no single place in London where all the big-crotch creatives live. Many collectors are based in Marylebone or Notting Hill. The spirits of Midas are concentrated on the same street just off Marylebone High Street, with sunnier homes elsewhere. Cy Twomblys for the Cyrenaic shore. Notting Hill is for slightly younger artsy types, a hauntology of nights spent at the Cow. My favourite Notting Hill film isn't *Notting Hill*. It's Horace Ové's *Pressure*. There are many close contenders, although there hasn't yet been a good film made in Notting Hill this century.

There are specific places in Notting Hill that guarantee zoo sightings of those with young moneyed voices, the most frustrating dead ringers in town, myself occasionally included. During my last visit to Kilgore, Sutter Kane, owner of a fashionable members' club, said he will soon sell the establishment and become a horror novelist. Lay low, lay him, or let him. Kilgore is just one of the many places where words are spoken with dumb lips and averted faces, searching for those more affluent in a room where girandoles decorate ornate corridors for nymphs from Horace and coquette coiffures. How refined to lean back in a chair during such occasions and ask *is that so*? The multiple scenes of affluence across the city are distinct from each other, like the different friendship groups in old American war buddy films. Men really went from GI to IG. Shoreditch is no longer cool — you don't feel so trapped inside an Aesop bubble. Wash your hands, put on your summer dress, look not so pale. Even the gentrifiers in Shoreditch are getting gentrified now. Huntingdon Estate, where a few East London galleries began, is being ripped down. A food court is being replaced with skyscrapers. There's 'save our food court' stickers on street lamps.

Paralysis and entrapment, the main themes of both Joyce's *Dubliners* and my new life in a different social universe. In my earlier years, Notting Hill said carnival to me, now it says vegan, gluten-free, low-carb cookies. Developed many allergies in the past two years. It was my body's reaction to a new life north of the river. Flat-white culture has spilled across the city, although most of the population manage to ignore it and maintain normal lives in the same area. There is something creatively stifling about flat-white culture, which is inescapable if you're in the art world, although it likely doesn't bother those who haven't known anything else. Many people who grew up in the art world don't even realise they live in a self-referential bubble. That referring to the art industry in an art practice is not referring to culture. That culture exists in its multitudes outside of the art world, first and foremost. They all seemed to have distant fathers who allowed them to run riot, whereas immigrant dads will literally try and get their kids arrested. That's the thing about London — you can be intimate with the city but in a new social circle you can find it unrecognisable. Depending on who you are, who you choose to become. It's not uncommon for certain streets my feet have walked for twenty years to feel suddenly unfamiliar. They first stepped into a gallery at eighteen years old. A friend told me that he, too, didn't come from the art world. So how did you end up wanting to be a gallerist? When we had dinner with Sadie Coles at our house in Hydra. My parents weren't even very big collectors, he added. Didn't know what to say. The mere thought of failing my parents, who sacrificed everything to give me a decent life, fills me with nausea. The third most Googled entry after my name is parents, although my dad is olive oil Arab, not oil money Arab. He fled a war and, by working around the clock, built a stable life with my mum. We socially mobilised into an aspirational middle-class family. That's an achievement that usually takes generations. My dad has a tremor in his hands. His discipline is my greatest inheritance. In the upper echelons of the class system, there's a noticeable trend amongst young people to either hate their parents or never bring them up in conversation. The bigger the denial, the bigger the trust fund.

There is a cushy complacency tied to the creative class of flat-white culture, which feels like taking a Xanax in the airport. You just have to cut through it. Even if you acquire an upper-class lifestyle, try not to succumb to the upper-class gaze. It is imperative to maintain the drive to hustle and work harder, even when you unlock a new level of comfort. Especially when there is less to fall back on. Successful elderly gallerists have endless drive, they work and travel constantly. But they're of a different generation. The creatively inclined in my generation have, deservedly or not, acquired a reputation for laziness. But presumably every generation prior had lazy people, we just never hear about them. Protect your time from men in Salomon XT6s and Arc'teryx softshell beanies. Ignore the ancient monoliths stuffed into their Dickies carpenter pants. Carrying my father's demonic work ethic, feeling the ancestral guilt that accompanies lie-ins and matcha. The infrastructure of upper-class 'culture' lived by the young and freelance class of East London is concentrated around townhouses in De Beauvoir and London Fields, quaint terraced houses behind Columbia Road and, increasingly, Farringdon. Those who entered creative industries to avoid a nine to five now work 24/7. All the girls who moved to Hackney have digestion problems. Even Samira yaps on about her gut health, since some twink made a comment about the size of our hips (derogatory). Luckily, she grew up with Arab aunties. These gays can't hurt her. Gentrifier culture is digested into the body: heirloom tomatoes, orange wine, Nocellara olives, chicken bone broth, raw ginger, sea moss, loose almonds, hummus crisps, asparagus, niche hot sauce brand and salt of tears. Never trust a man who cried over the death of Anthony Bourdain.

Across the city wealthy people announce their presence through subtle idiosyncrasies. Putting ice cubes into a glass of expensive white wine. Not looking at the bill before they pay. Preferring a hidden local gem to a Michelin-starred restaurant. Not snapping spaghetti before cooking it. An iPhone weather app listing London, Paris, New York, Milan, Hydra and Gstaad. Symptomatic of life in a sprawling city, Londoners tend to hook up on the basis of geographical proximity, a filter available on dating apps, which once commodified dating and now commodify dissatisfaction with dating.

The place you choose to settle in the city and the areas you frequent are often used to sketch an entire existence. Generally, it is difficult now to be received in a way that permits duality and contradiction, despite that being an ongoing condition of existence for those of us ethnically bound to the so-called Global South. Your people are dying and you're eating risotto at Bice after sitting front row at a runway in Milan. *How dare you.* What's considered trashy if you're poor but chic if you're rich? Speaking multiple languages and tax avoidance. A life lesson in code-switching. Guilty, an Ossian in a hessian Loewe sunhat. Call me a foxymoron. Gold chain around my neck so fair, and rhyming gamely with John Clare. Why are women born into generational wealth always flat-chested? The maintenance of a luxurious lifestyle and liberal politics is termed champagne socialism, older sister of the trust-fund goth, the revolutionary-in-residence libbing out on a grassroots arts residency in Dulwich. Putting the fun in funding. The middle class have overtaken the left. Liberalism: the weaponisation of leftist slogans to mask deeply conservative actions. Merely critiquing the far right has somehow become a political end goal. Another crisis of the left is our inability to have nuanced conversations. It's just like, you're morally wrong, and if you have a different opinion to me, shut up. Hopefully we grow out of it. Anyhow, men are out here lying, the evidence is in their throats. Adam probably had a big snooker stick too, BDE in BCE.

Many people in the art world harbour a fetish for proximity to the 'realness' that permeated my childhood. This realisation helped me understand, as an adult, where true value lies and will always lie. We can't let cultural value be determined by a bunch of nepo babies who've never been to a real party. Generationally wealthy people tend to romanticise the working classes and cultivate disdain for the middle classes, if they have any consciousness of class at all. They love a stinky lunchbox story. If exceedingly rich people become bored and strive for something beyond their moneyed orbit, they are often disingenuous about it. Regular perpetrators include upper-class white women in the white waters of midlife and looking for a cause. It's one thing to become interested in another community's struggle, and another to claim authority within that struggle without fully attempting to join that community, without having experienced any of the struggle. It is better than racism, but still jarring. There is a fine line between solidarity and whitesplaining. Such as whenever well-meaning white people imagine they are us and mistake it for solidarity. Arab on their friend's side.

For example, a socialite converting to Islam is mildly interesting, while their in-built entitlement makes it all too probable they will end up whitesplaining Ghassan Kanafani to you on a sun lounger at Il Pellicano. You would be surprised by how many privileged white women, sustained by divorce settlements, spend one season in North Africa only to start sprinkling *bess* and *la* into their sentences; all the time criticising people for not being politically outspoken enough. She won't check herself, because as far as she's aware, it's now her struggle too, she's part of our community, and we are her polite hosts.

Luxury is a wellspring of aspiration. Me and my mum used to take the train into Central to visit the designer shops on Old Bond Street and see the new season collections en *Vogue* in person. My older brothers never wanted to come. My mum used to stand outside and wait for me. Everything was beyond my means, but still it was essential we visit all the stores. Little could get in the way of my curiosity. The ladies who could afford these shops also had access to this thing called artwork, which many take to be another kind of luxury product. Luxury was redefined by French conglomerates, who put aside their ideals of haute couture and appropriated streetwear. Venerable fashion houses became the profitable loci of aspirational logo products. They made billions. The French have always been the most astute colonisers.

The global elite have a keen intellectual and cultural interest in people of the lowest socioeconomic stratum, but a significant indifference otherwise. Sure, most people in the art world would disagree, particularly those who have friends of colour. However, these friends are almost always celebrities or from the upper class. This indifference is violent and infuriating. Those who infiltrate the global elite are artists who often deal with violence in an academic format deemed acceptable by the art world. A whitewashing of trauma performed by minorities through a minimalist Félix González-Torres aesthetic. Similarly, angsty aesthetic gestures have taken the place of real trauma, as developed by artists such as Nan Goldin. Many art students nowadays make Nan Goldin–style work without experiencing a fraction of her pain. This extends to how people dress today according to music subcultures without engagement beyond the aesthetic. *Welcome to the desert of the real.*

It felt sobering to cycle to Holland Park, where Leila grew up. Leila is a jewellery designer and an art collector. She had decided to throw an impromptu gathering for her old friend, an Iranian art editor visiting from the Lower Beast Side. New York slander is one of my favourite conversation topics because people get so worked up about it. But without growing up there, it's hard to see what all the fuss is about. Then again, the only community accessible for me in Manhattan is bumping into someone vaguely recognisable from the art world outside Saint Ambrose or the Odeon. Which explains my feelings about New York. Community formed primarily on the basis of shared access to wealth is a questionable entry point of community. Leila's house is located in a curve of cream mansions, similar to Park Crescent, although no-one interesting lives on Park Crescent.

Bonjour alaykum, darling, Leila greeted me at the door, giving mob wife in a vintage fur coat. My early arrival was met with a flurry of chefs, waiters and nannies, who whisked, poured and stirred. The violin played like a catgut thong. Leila instructed me to go speak with the chef, who was Iraqi and grew up in Grenfell Tower, as she ran out on a last-minute errand. The chef looked stressed. *His line was stressed.* Remember when being stressed used to just mean squeezing a stress ball? Not ayahuasca breath-work

CBD MDMA journal-therapy guided-sound bath mushrooms. Before any opportunity to distract the chef, Leila's six young children ran down the stairs and wrapped their arms around the distressed knees of my jeans and kneecaps of soft star-flames.

The eldest gave me a detailed account of her school day. What was your favourite part? Latin class. My least favourite part of the day is sleeping alone. The tragedy of bedsheets empty, sheets of writing paper full. There are many days when Caleb does not come home and instead works all night in his studio. That way he can wake up early with no distractions, to more easily begin making work again, before his studio team arrive. During the day, he ends up being more of a manager. Then he'll unexpectedly come home and lie down, flesh smudged, on our bed. We lie upright, his hands sew a painting and mine flick through a novel. Entangled bodies forming wonky letters on linen sheets. Fall asleep, his stomach my pillow of cool flesh. She lay on him, caressing her own tomb. Caleb is always painting, and when we go to Birkin bag restaurants he draws me on the tablecloth or napkin. The doorbell buzzed me out of my thoughts.

The first official guest to arrive at Leila's home was a childhood friend of her cousin. They went to Eton together. He was the Moncler mountaineering type who decided to swap the Amazon offices for the Amazon rainforest. He scrolled rapidly through his camera roll and showed me his bachelor chalet in Bern, the birthplace of Robert Walser. It looked like the mountains on Evian bottles. He came with an economics professor from Oxford who played padel and had the personality of an arthritic greyhound. The G7 Summit is *Sex and the City* for finance bros. What's your favourite position? CEO. Personalities poured forth and huddled together murmuring. The party's guest of honour made a silent entrance. She spoke quietly as if straining to hear the Earth turn, cutting through small talk with humbleness and wisdom, a Solomon in Salomon trainers. Down to earth, a creative perigee surrounded by pedigree.

Still hungover from the night before, my body flopped down in a corner with two friends, Langston and Mehdi. They're the meridian of socialites and hard-working people, which is a balancing act. Like losing weight and gaining muscle, but in the art world. Or gossiping while maintaining discretion. We chatted lazily and picked at the diluvial debris of dairy from cheeseboards sliding off our laps. Langston was hungover. He was out last night with an art advisor, who turned out to be an elevated scammer. In the art world, regret usually comes from being caught, rather than remorse for committing a crime. We discussed Langston's upcoming ceramics exhibition, as well as the trials and tribulations of this and that member of the British gentry. There are many socialites who are extremely hard-working, but then they are not known first and foremost as socialites. It is a term reserved for the Daisy Buchanans of this world. The most tolerable of these socialites languish in pure opulence, the old-school type who don't pretend to be anything else. The young European socialites in

London all loosely engage with social justice causes but are actually influencers, without wanting to appear as such. Most are signed to the Kate Moss Agency. They all act a little bit gothic. The infantry of nepo babies in the art world often establish their own galleries, opening the doors to their parents' clients and wealthy friends. Or they feign to work by creating titles for themselves within their parents' galleries, organising special projects so special they never happen. People mistake effort for achievement. Some socialites have a penchant for reading and make it their entire personality and start a book club. We're in a generation where everyone feels the need to scale up or monetise their hobbies. How about just having a hobby and enjoying being bad at it?

A paragraph for the length of time it takes to smoke a cigarette: the beauty of socialites lies in their ability to build beautiful lives. These often become the blueprint for aspiration, packaged and peddled by fashion brands. They all look so good, these socialite women. All mesmerising. They spend significant time and money cultivating their beauty. It is something they really think about, which is quite romantic. Some turn it into a job. This ability to fabricate a beguiling existence for themselves, the type of life falsely imitated by influencers on social media, is what draws people to them. Being off social media is a privilege afforded to well-connected people. These young socialites who do not feel suffocated by their existence but manage to embrace it. My entry into this world piqued the interest of many older socialite women, esteemed clitterati, who sometimes gossip about each other to me, being all avuncular, pulling out receipts dated decades ago, because their secrets remain secrets with me. We speak to each other but it's often not as sophisticated as what in novels is termed conversation, where dialogue always seems to be contrived with a purpose, often to do with advancing the vertiginous arc of a plot. Whispers are exchanged, a grave discourse of who fucks who, and who does worse. My newness is probably what sparks their oversharing, or maybe they do that to everyone on the margins, since they're probably all bored of each other.

Leila has told me many times not to trust any of them, and that spending time with other socialites yields more nothingness. Leila is Palestinian, so our relationship is different; we share an intrinsic and deep-seated trust from our belonging to another community. The massacre is the message. As for the specific world we live in, in London? There has never been any question of whether either of us belong. We belong. The question is how. How do we want to belong to that world, outside of the parameters it has already drawn for us? Leila's warnings have not ended my fascination with the glamour of socialites, their true elegance. Besides, she is one of them. And she isn't twenty-three years old, like me. Whatever. It will probably wear off with time. Miniskirted around the coffee table and flicked through a back issue of *The Gentlewoman*. Why do Roy and Dorothy Lichtenstein look like every couple on Feeld? My fingers plucked Elizabeth Hardwick's novel *Sleepless Nights* from the wall of books behind me. Placed it between the slope of swan neck and shoulder, for use as a pillow. Bought a copy soon after. They didn't have it in any of the Hackney public libraries. Grew up going to the library, chain-reading Anaïs Nin between the bedsheets of book covers. Moving beyond talk of socialites, scanning the bookshelves, we discussed existentialist classics like *The Stranger* and *The Real Housewives of Potomac* until we began to fall asleep on the sofa. Love our falling asleep moment. Survive by keeping your eyes open, lash and lid.

Pushing vertical, my limbs transported themselves to the next function, snared by the sound of drums. It was a small concert in an artist's studio in Whitechapel, her first live performance. She is predominantly known as a painter — a visual arts painter, not a house painter — that mysterious profession of wrist veins coursing with limpid vision. The room was full of people, mainly British people, who become oddly paralysed when they hear live music, arms glued to their sides and limp heads of hair nodding in agreement to an invisible question. Fentanyl fairies mouthing air, mindlessly recording horizontal videos of the performances with 16:9 supremacy. The girls chant Dua Lipa instead of duaas. A freelance scene reporter from a new online art magazine kept harassing people for hot takes. He came up to me. My hot take? There is no difference between history and fiction anymore. People will learn this the hard way in the second part of the century. What do you mean? Well — Omg did you see Lindsay Lohan's new face? This was the first time many of the vulture capitalists had ventured to the area. Caleb found me in the crowd.

He held what he called a perfect coffee. It was made on a La Marzocco machine with Climpson & Sons beans. How did you get from Holland Park to Whitechapel so fast? It's a short novel. Afterwards we walked quickly to his studio building nearby. Overtook an elderly lady. Agilitymogging. Caleb's phone rang and he spoke into it, ignoring me. Hang on a minute, Tim. He looked at me. Tell them about your childhood, he said, so they can get to know you. Tell them until the end of my call. It will add to your character. He resumed his call.

Exposition. Whitechapel reminds me in ways of another version of the city, of growing up in Croydon. Although less in Croydon, more on the internet. Caroused through Whitgift Centre with school friends wearing Jane Norman and side fringes, dramatically flipping LG Cookie phones, swinging our charms, tossing around Paul's Boutique handbags, growing up like blank pages being filled. Fruit winders and Monster Munch. Ringtones by M.I.A, Stormzy, Alesha Dixon, Alexandra Burke, Corinne Bailey Rae, Leona Lewis. Navy TOMS. KEEP CALM AND CARRY ON. Ice bucket challenge. Food-heated faces from McDonald's and smelling of Dior Sauvage. Every boy went to college to study sports science. The best of my education came from schoolmaster Red Hanrahan. The rest of my literary education? Reading every poet mentioned in Roberto Bolaño's *The Savage Detectives*. Listening to every episode of Michael Silverblatt's *Bookworm*. The riots in 2011 marked a shift in the area, and the authorities used it as an excuse to push forward with gentrification. In the second of Virgil's *Eclogues*, Corydon was a goatherd who loved a boy. Gay pastoral is an incongruous reference point for the borough. My parents did their best to protect me from the worst of the city, a reasonable impulse that felt like stifling constraint to a teenager. Protection these days comes with socialising in circles of extreme privilege and associating with a specific whiteness that will never feel like home. My parents' strictness kept me on a certain path oriented towards building a secure life. Sewing kits in the biscuit tin, frozen kibbeh from visiting uncles, good china behind the cabinet glass. My only trip through Croydon nowadays is the occasional journey to Gatwick Airport, during which a cab driver with rheumatic wheels might take a route passing by my old dentist clinic, the chippy we went on Friday nights, and Wing Yip, where my dad used to buy moon cakes after Sunday mass. The amount of labour done by other people to get me here is crazy. Maybe I'll be able to spend time there again in a few years, but it's all still too fresh.

In the infancy of the twenty-first century — my infancy — we arrived in the UK. The first thing my brothers did was try every single cake in Patisserie Valerie. Three girls used to corner me in the bathroom at primary school and bully me into saying certain words in my accent. Still can't eat custard because it reminds me of school dinners. As do bread and butter pudding and sticky toffee pudding. Rounders, scared of the hard ball. The coloured stickers that teachers assigned to each book, according to difficulty level. You couldn't read what you wanted. Confined to Michael Morpurgo and

Jacqueline Wilson. Streaming Sonic Youth on Grooveshark. Peak Vine. My name is Noah. How you doing? Don't fucking touch me or I'm suing. Quick trips on my scooter to Woolworths after school. Major family events celebrated at a Zizzi restaurant. My piano teacher had arthritis. She kept telling me to get rid of my long fake nails. Tried to keep the burglar away on *The Sims*. Bought an Abercrombie polo shirt while visiting family in America. My bullies accused me of wearing a fake, because it was baggy. The baggier men's version was just cooler. Glow bracelets at the school disco. Paired with 3D cinema glasses – the lenses popped out – and a moustache necklace. An older boy in a Kenzo jumper and Superdry puffer said he rated me for sitting down. The next day he poked me on Facebook.

Screen memories. MSN usernames, Hotmail email accounts. 3D Pinball Space Cadet. Tamagotchi pets. Club Penguin. Crazy Walker's crisp flavours. Guinea pigs, named Ant and Dec. Ears pierced at Claire's. Fake Heelys from Amman. JLS, fancied Marvin. (You had to fancy one.) Geography teacher with rotten teeth from smoking. Won a school poetry competition. Lost a school short story competition. (No beginning, middle, or end.) Clarks shoes, but not with the dolls inside. *Alvin and the Chipmunks* songs on YouTube. The Arab Spring on YouTube. Group trips to newly opened Westfield. Hollister, frozen yoghurt boom, Nando's all the time. Chippy tea. Fancy dinners with Shloer. School play, school photo. Designer from TK Maxx. National Book Tokens. My auntie still buys me them for my birthday. Kesha on mp3 player. Beyoncé on pink iPod nano. First CD? Ne-Yo's *Year of the Gentleman.* Sang it on my pink karaoke machine. The Boxing Day holiday sales, my parents booking all their flights one year in advance. Dad bringing us cut fruit when studying. Mum doing zumba on the TV. She wore Paul Costello on special occasions. Always with a Michael Kors bag. Dad driving her mad by flipping through TV channels during ad breaks, because they were too long.

Sat cross-legged so close to the TV the static tickled my nose. A strange child: less infant, more outfant. Mum gossiping on the landline to her sister about *Emmerdale*. The antiquity of a home phone. Her favourite actor Patrick Swayze died one day when she was driving me to school. Capital Summertime Ball. Major. Can't remember my friends or their names. Thank you, mum and dad. Tears of gratitude. Memory, why torment me? The only true clarity left in this city is the barking of dogs.

Caleb's new studio is a magical skip. He just bought it. He is waiting for local planning permissions to begin renovation. To navigate the building, you have to crouch below hanging wires, duck plaster piñatas, and sidestep debris. Caleb doesn't read novels, which means writing has always felt mine, possessively mine. He probably won't even read this. He doesn't read much, although he reads well. My interest in his work is more active. He has taught me a hell of a lot about art, more than my art history degrees. His building was a school, once. One lecture room for students is still intact, an installation with wooden bleachers, demonstration table, and antique markings, carved timelessly by bored Edwardian students. Opiated and opinionated. Romy, he called me by name. A girl like you is hard to find. Huh, but not harder to find than a good gluten-free pizza base.

We decided to fuck in the classroom, our inaugural sex act in the new building, a beatitude of cum stains added to the bygone spillages on the wooden table; a sum of cum. He opened my legs as wide as demand-induced scarcity and gave me head. I lay naked on the teacher's desk, face turned to the empty benches, listening to moans of ghosts that moved us in a variety of rhythms. He had a school of hands which touched everywhere with hard grips and light caresses. Many mouths, wings of fleshy lips brushing so swiftly past mine. Liquid love flooded every orifice, anticipation fingered to climax. His words carried colours with sounds penetrating flesh. *Romances sans paroles*, wrote Paul Verlaine.

Together on paper
we work to make
our bodies meet,
your paintbrush
my pen, saint of write,
or wrong, paint and pain,
when our bodies move.
Together on paper,
our shared images
our fingerprints
your body writes into
my flesh.

This poem
paints us, we made us
our idea, heavy with
love, paperweight.

Beyond here, words don't go.

5

The night turned into Monday, which is a terrible thing. The foghorn of bin lorries woke the drowsy rats and me. Stared at the ceiling and turned onto my left side, which migrated a migraine across my temples and unblocked my right nostril. Stalled an early morning of emails by staying in bed doomscrolling through hauls from the Chloë Sevigny yard sale. My hot take is that one day tech abstinence will become commonplace for the upper classes — specifically, those running the tech companies — as they instead become one with nature, while their dopamine loops ravage and enslave the lower classes. Who could've guessed that the villains of this century would be protein fiends in blue shirts and On Running trainers? My nighttimes have begun to eclipse daytimes, which is never good for productive thesis editing. It would be different if my work stakes were in the art world, for then my nighttime activities would be work obligations. Becoming an artist or a gallerist will never be on the cards. My point has yet to be found. Jonas Mekas—one of my heroes—made films, wrote, and ran Anthology Film Archives. Bradley Eros told me he used to live under the seats of the Maya Deren Theatre. My future is not as a girlboss CEO. That much has become clear. My excitement stems from watching films and reading, not listening to Bloomberg podcasts. For now, my focus is on partying in the pursuit of fun. There is a craic epidemic. And there is the curiosity to learn about my new world. Our day will come. Fade away, dissolve and forget the weariness, resolve. Opening, dinner, party.

As confidence grows, it will soon be time to figure out how to be more myself in this world, rather than attempting to assimilate and self-annihilate. To make more of this life and to make more of it mine, with enough Irishness to remain grounded. Dreaming of a time when each new room no longer warrants the need to explain my presence, shaking off social burdens of the party girl, the girlfriend-of, the something-to-do-with-film. The writer-who-hasn't-written-anything-yet role. To be or not to be, that is the infinitive phrase. The Dazed 100 to Forbes 30 Under 30 pipeline. Me? Been on them all before twenty-three years old. Romy is successful, but no-one knows at what. It is important to know the threshold of your differences within this world. Mine relates to specific political world views that are not shared so widely in the art industry. We're in an epoch of fiction over fact, which is bad politically, but good literarily. Politics are rarely a topic of conversation at art-world dinners, as if the people who buy art were not also those who rule the world.

Last month I sat next to the wife of a CEO of a major pharmaceutical company, who said she didn't believe in the Labour Party or the Conservative Party, she just believed in parties. Her husband put her heart in a climate-controlled storage unit and flipped it five months later. Grace is learning to join people at a place of difference, with an open heart. Caleb's snoring went from pianissimo to fortissimo and interrupted my musings. He lay on his stomach with arms stretched across the bed in a landscape. Performed a sickle motion with my thighs wrapped around his body. Flanks on flanks. RIP Karl Marx, you would have loved me.

Endured video meetings that could have been emails. Touched a heaviness behind my forehead as if something was in there. Between meetings my eyeballs scrolled through TikTok. My brain on aeroplane mode. Circled my garret in an open robe with phone wedged between ear and shoulder, speaking past an unlit cigarette affixed to my lip gloss. Admin days invoke feelings of restlessness and loneliness. Faffing about. Drifting like a celluloid siren without her script. Watched a Letterboxd critic asking a famous actress about her views on abortion. It's anti-feminist, she replied vaguely, with a scholastic air. Millennial pause, standing applause. She'll be proclaimed a feminist tomorrow. Criticism in the art world is often found in reviews, which sometimes make the art more complex than it is, and other times, more understandable, more . . . sellable. Art wants you to see like it sees. Drifting thoughts worthy of Leopold Bloom, if he had a twenty-four-inch waist. Drifting whilst pondering whether we should continue to measure time in days as the primary measure of time for everyone, forever. It would be better to live by love because it is easier to remember a kiss than a day. Drowsy thoughts: my mind drifted to food. Conjured literary images of venison roasted on a smoky spit and the delicious chocolate bars from Jean-Pierre Crévin. Hôtel Costes in Paris leaves them on pillows, a hotel near Place Vendôme that looks like the velvet pouch of a jewellery display case. Their rooms are cosy and make one feel as if they are inside a vagina, cervix the widening gyre.

Took a quick break in the afternoon for a cuppa and found pleasure in slowly removing the bloated Barry's tea bag from a giant Sports Direct mug. Babe, tea and coffee is everything. Go on, put the kettle on. It's the right point in the story for it. Reading a book feels like streaming a film. You can decide when to stop and to resume. My mind drifted lazily to cinematic images: blood dripping on snow. Eve Babitz wrote that Francis Ford Coppola never ate on Mondays. Who? What? Six-seven. Hunger eventually exceeded the capacity for me to make any sense. Cooking in the late afternoon without having eaten all day makes me a satanic housewife. Fisting a turkey, seasoned with onion powder, cooked with the heat of hell. Avid poetry reader, ulyssesly bad cook. Fabergé eggs fried by Pan. Gentrifryer. More *Simple Life* than trad wife. It takes a long time for my admin-induced restlessness to wear off. Admin kills my brain so much it becomes impossible to extract even one metaphor from the pantomime of a sunset outside my window. Grab a sunset and crunch it in your hand. It is imperative to continue working so there is no need to repeat an admin day tomorrow. Favourite fruit? Apple Pay. Then, loneliness kicks in.

The end of admin day. Completed tasks vanished below the horizon, my sanity with them. One of my friends had reserved a table at some new supper club but he felt dizzy during a studio visit and cancelled. There was a back-up friend scheduled, we were raped at the same age. But he said he was shooting, either heroin, a film, or clay pigeons. He recently moved to the country to protect his skin barrier. The worst thing to do after a long admin day is to be alone, because it results in the Gen Z phenomenon of spiralling. The scrolling classes want to make quick money from passive income. No shade. Many have seen their parents grind endlessly at state jobs for decades, and for what? Growing up, my parents taught me that it is important to get a job for the primary reasons of making money and attaining stability. Since observing friends from the upper classes, it has become possible to imagine choosing what to do in life for the sole fact of it being desirable, before it is immediately profitable. This is called chasing a dream, the antonym of life lessons learned from my parents' class.

My wilting body lugged itself to small Tesco in a quest for a pint of milk, too deflated to walk just slightly further to The Supermarket, an upscale supermarket with girl snacks. Little-treat culture arises from the fact that most young people will never be able to afford property. So, disposable income goes on dumb shit instead, in twenty-first-century colours. Caroused around crunching into an apple, a costard on Co-Star. Is this chocolate slave-free? My outfit for small Tesco was a stained t-shirt that said *BITCH*. There is an excellent photograph of me wearing it next to Cicciolina at a fashion show in Milan. My greasy hair was wrapped in a Hermès foulard, concealing a bare face of self-loathing. Poached eyes in a boiled head. Period blood dripped from my vagina like cold-pressed cranberry juice from an expensive kitchen appliance.

In small Tesco my feeling of loneliness began to stretch longer than the M25. But the feeling soon disappeared because being in a city means bumping into a whole village any time you leave the house, whether you want to or not. The belly of this beast is bloated with parties. Bumped into Tom, who was just at The Supermarket, armed with enough organic products to cook our privilege. He invited me for dinner, which cured my decision paralysis and led to a leisurely evening walk along the canal with my pint of milk. People need to stop fucking cycling along the canal. Waved at a magpie. There was a long queue for Towpath. Saw a man turn to look back at a BBL, and he turned into a pillar of salt. Lot's wife with a lot of arse. Strolled past a fishmonger and patted the little silver heads with the pad of my index finger. Jumped in all of the puddles. Stomped further in my wet loafers with a fistful of angry tulips. Stopped to observe grey clouds of rose incense beside dew-cold lilies. Dried figs and wild honey scented the air. Passed the new climbing gym co-working space. A short man accidentally spilled scalding coffee over his hand. The singeing singing pain made his hand shrink into a fist of fingers in palm, a palsy of pain which in shame and rage passed a searing scream from his throat to his mouth to the outside world. Looked up and dispatched my head on an upwards journey, towards that cyclops called the sun. Sinewy veins of aircraft contrails shot across the sky, stamped with clouds and the steel beanstalks of skyscraper construction sites, some inner-city remix of a fairytale.

Tom's house felt desperately lonely, because he still had no furniture aside from a lamp he bought from the Pistachio Vendor. Positioned next to Emahoy Tsege Mariam Gebru vinyls. Perhaps my air of loneliness is projected onto Tom. He doesn't understand my loneliness. You have Caleb. Yes, but occasionally he locks himself in his studio for weeks on end. Although he takes me on tons of dates. William Blake's nobodaddy, my Nobudaddy. My loneliness comes from being constantly surrounded by people, always at a slightly self-enforced distance. Writing is a good type of loneliness because you don't need anyone else to do it. In the city, writing is a rare activity in which you can be completely alone. Even when you're surrounded by people, in your own head. Most novelists must be alone all the time, because you never see them at parties. Except for Deborah Levy, whenever she's in town. Maybe novelists attend different types of parties. Are there book-world parties? A novelist sat front row at a JW Anderson show this season. What's in a name? A book deal. Giuseppe Bertini made a Dante-themed stained-glass window at the Museo Poldi Pezzoli, which, at the time, probably had the same prestige as guest-editing an issue of the *Financial Times' How to Spend It* supplement. It is possible to be visible but to give little of yourself. Andy Warhol had a doorstop diary, but he didn't give much away.

While listening to my ruminations, Tom put away the groceries weighing down his netted shopping bags, they looked like Eva Hesse sculptures. He cooked me an Irish stew, which balanced on a table of my knees, crossed on the yoga mat carpeting uneven wooden floorboards. Put on a film whilst we eat. Tom scrolled through the titles leaving the Criterion Collection at the end of the month. We started watching a two-hour movie for a meal that took four minutes to eat. Tom, have you read *Mulligan Stew*? Huh? Accidentally knocked down a virginal pile of unread books. What if we knew each other by our knees? It's boring identifying people by their faces. And don't you think knuckles are like small knees?

We discussed my idea for a debut novel, my first time between covers. *Young British Fags* (*YBFs*). Wait, that can't be the title, Tom said. We can't just exist in the shadow of the YBAs. None of the YBAs even want to be called YBAs. They hate the term. And many artists were retrospectively left out, like Hamad Butt. Alright. Well, regardless, it will be a very fictional novel. You'll be fiction, Teddy will be fi— Fiction! Why? That's just a bullshit cover. Like a sort of cringe fancy dress. All that pretending. Since when did you become a pussy? Trust me, Tom, you'll thank me later. (He did.) His life is a fact, which has no place in fiction. Besides, there can be emotional truth in fiction. You can be personal without being autobiographical. Don't worry, it will toe the line. The exposition: a young 'other' woman becomes an adult and discovers her contradictions. Her new adult world doesn't share the same values. She struggles to let go of who she used to be and to hold on to both realities, whilst figuring out who she wants to become. Tom rolled his eyes. Well, Romy, your writing would be better if you allowed yourself to reflect or feel something. No, you're wrong. There are too many feelings, that's why they're pushed down. The surface is emotional. We spend more time on the surface than in the depths of our emotions anyway.

Changed the title to *Scene City*. There will be no plot, people will keep reading for the vibe. Like a finished version of Truman Capote's *Answered Prayers*. But less bitchy, more cunty. Who will you be? Tom asked. The narrative voice. Main character energy. Maybe named Paige because it sounds like page. Ha ha. That's dumb, Tom said. What about . . . Romy? Like Romy Schneider? No, like the nepo baby. Since that is what everyone thinks you are. Romy Mars, Sofia Coppola's daughter? No, the other one. Pause. Romy David, Larry David's daughter? What? No. Whatever. Nepo babies are born, you are made. Having a character is important for an author to hide behind, even if these days readers tend to vilify *the author* for creating *fictional characters* who have *problematic beliefs*. All the characters rolled their eyes, even those who weren't on this page.

My character is role-playing as author, your character as reader. You listen to me, you criticise me, you tell me to shut up. As my friends, you already do all the things a reader should do. Do readers have input on the characters? Absolutely not. You're not even my ideal readers, to be honest. Especially Teddy, who just reads for entertainment. But you're the readers of my life, so you're the ones I'm stuck with. I'm also stuck with representation, but you can't write a novel without it. Well, you could, but . . . *Scene City* needs to mean something to you. Because I care about you, I really do. You give me meaning. So you're controlling us, using us to serve your own artistic vision, and expecting us to give you meaning, without pay? Cut it out, Tom. You're a fiction of my imagination. So is everyone else in the group chat. No, we're not. Well, of course you don't think you are, because you are all characters . . . What about if I call you my muse, does that feel better? You can have your own interiority, off the page. Do whatever you want with it. Just try not to let it affect your presence here too much. That's why I want to be a novelist, so I can work alone, unlike in theatre or film, where you need a lot of people to make it happen. You sound like a villainous studio executive talking about their newly signed AI musician. Well, fiction is literally about feeling real things for fake people. Characters. Point being, if my characters are going to act up, well, I'll kill us all, I'll — Compose yourself. What else do you think I'm doing?

Move on, Tom sighed. Well, the city will be the protagonist, and its characters will be flattened, with lots of style. The phrase 'all style, no substance' is bullshit. Of course, people in the British book world only say it because they all dress terribly. Style has substance. But as a society, we're running out of style. Our modernist buildings were once made as an image of the future, but now they're in desperate need of renovation. Same goes for the modern novel. Nothing feels more old-fashioned nowadays than a modernist. We recycle history's blasphemies and make them sacred again . . . Conversation wiped across surfaces, disinfecting our dirty talk. This was hanging out, my brain rot was excused.

We discussed the final season of *Succession* and deliberated who would inherit Dérosian, the kingpin of mega art galleries. We saw Levi Dérosian recently at Claridge's. He was on his way to Basel. He still has a twinkle in his eye. Many of the historically important art dealers have become figureheads of their eponymous mega galleries. Many emerging artists who joined mega galleries straight out of school had their work priced too high, too soon, which is not sustainable for a long-term career. It can also become a challenge if an artist's upcoming exhibition doesn't look anything like their previous one. A new body of work necessitates building a new market. There never used to be a problem for the names on the door, but many of the risk-taking figureheads who established the most-esteemed galleries are now in their eighties and understandably less active with the younger artists on their programmes. The directors working under them are often better at maintaining the brands of artists with single notable bodies of work. This is all very well for artists who prefer to make one type of signature work, as many famous ones do, without needing to diversify their market. A great idea is impossible, so, if you figure one out, you may as well stick with it. I was my mother's great idea. She thought, therefore I was. Authors have great ideas that become signatures, too. Baudelaire's spleen, Leopardi's ennui, Kirkegaard's fear and trembling, Mallarmé's purism.

Smacked my lips together. One day they'll say: Romy's lip gloss. The concept of the mega gallery is dying. The next era will be more about regionalisation, being hands-on with artists, and building a specific community. Value will return to the artist. The art world is extremely social, either way. Deals are made with collectors during lunches and parties and holidays on obscure Cycladic islands. But the sociality of the rest of it — mainly the never-ending stream of openings — is relentless. Openings are often just a huge expense for the gallery, with no financial benefit, because good collectors buy without all the palaver. The soft surcease of tattle allowed us to move on.

Here are the makings of an early twenty-first-century evening. The end of the millennium is now distant. Tom asked me if WWIII was going to happen. It's basically already happening. His mind jumps around like mine. Don't you think Bill Viola looks like Steve Jobs? Tom asked. Perhaps it's the other way around. Do you love God or the images of God? God? I don't know him. Invited Tom to church with my family. My huge family. Like in *Rocco and His Brothers.* The most Arab non-Arab film ever. The gleam of gold and incense-laden air drowsing in a cloud of murmured prayer. Write a thousand sacraments and carry them in your palm. There's something gay about the swish of a soutane, a neck hung with a crucifix. Tom hates God but loves the disciples, a group of men who died for eternal love.

We strolled down Teesdale Street and inhaled its energy like some sort of tarmac diviners. Bumped into a few friends and listened to their qualms. He's sick of it. Of what? The whole gestalt of it. Oh. In 1927 Virginia Woolf wrote an essay titled 'Street Haunting' about strolling in London, which she said is most enjoyed in the winter between 4 and 6 p.m. Woolf was crying wolf. The most satisfactory time for a stroll is during the warmer months and after a hearty dinner, during the golden hour. Pity the men who cried *Woolf*. Our rambling was interrupted by the editor-in-chief of a big fashion magazine who phoned Tom and told us to join him for drinks at Elgin House. So off we went.

The place-to-be since the 2010s, Elgin House is a mid-century gale of celebrities and people who want to meet celebrities. The art world allows for maximum exposure to celebrities and minimum identification with them. The most publicly adored among them often have sensational publicists. In these Roaring '20s, Elgin House is also heavily populated with women who behave like celebrities, the type of influencer who aspires to marry someone rich in finance. They are more put-together than me: a blastula blob of messiness within a corporate world. Influencers tend to have none of the modesty evinced by people who are actually famous. Fame, that tea bag of a word, served in fine porcelain and strengthened when steeped over a long period. The editor-in-chief looked relieved when we arrived. He who had stars for his flock. He shortly retired, and left us with his dinner company, Luna and Noah Cohen.

Pop stars like Noah are interesting to me because they become emblematic of a specific era which they never actually get to experience, due to all the duties of being famous. Luna was dressed opulently for the editor — and any paparazzi – in custom-made Jean Paul Gaultier. She gets it custom, you're a customer. You, my dear, look like you just got dragged through a bush, Tom muttered, seeing me still dressed for small Tesco in my *BITCH* t-shirt with greasy hair and no makeup. Commendably, my fist still gripped the pint of milk. Wheyfaced. When you don't lead with your physical appearance, you just need to retain some vague awareness of it, so you don't let yourself go too much. Too late. This was partly a fault of mine, having failed to predict that my evening would involve an intimate dinner with the biggest celebrities on the planet.

Noah sweated obedience, a quixotic Quixote. His wife was sweet, even if using snail mucin was the only thing we shared in common. Luna wrote her skincare doctrine for me on a serviette, serving a femme catechism. There was an entire hermeneutics of character analysis in her routine. Every person is already a complex character with motives that we divine incorrectly. Pause. It's impossible to form a definitive opinion about someone you have only met once, especially celebrities, who must be exhausted by constantly keeping their social battery switched on. Our few hours' interaction didn't result in any further reflection on their characters. Meeting celebrities never makes me starstruck. They're usually quite boring. The fact that so many people are grossly fascinated by the lives of specific types of workers, particularly in the entertainment industry, baffles me. What if paparazzi one day began trailing a talented heart surgeon, instead of a talented pop singer? What makes the work of a pop singer so interesting that it warrants an obsession with every minute detail of their life? Celebrity culture can be seen as serving to rationalise the gap between rich and poor. Someone has probably already written about that. Regardless, my extensive skincare knowledge has prepared me to hold long conversations with celebrity influencers like Luna. My routine is scrupulous and reads like a poem:

> 'She Walks in Beauty' (Revised) (1814)
> Lord Byron ft. Romy H____.
>
> Anua Cleansing Oil
> CeraVe Cleanser
> Round Lab Dodko Toner
> Haruharu Wonder Black Rice Hyaluronic Toner
> Cosrx Snail Mucin Essence
> SkinCeuticals CE Ferulic
> COSRX Advanced Snail Peptide Eye Cream
> Aestura Atobarrier365 Cream
> Beauty of Joseon Relief Sunscreen
>
> Sent from my iPhone

If Oppenheimer had been a girl my morning skincare routine would be the atomic bomb. There were not enough collective brain cells on the table to extend our conversation beyond skincare. Throughout the entire evening our companions didn't ask Tom or me one single question. Luna was happy only speaking about herself, perhaps without even realising she was doing it. She was comfortable only with the fact we were held in some sort of regard by the editor-in-chief whom she wanted to impress. She chirped about her brand while sipping on a porn star martini and had a habit of glancing upwards, like a perverse Madonna. It is always a strange experience to share an evening with people who give you their time but show no interest in getting to know you. Caleb reckons that such behaviour is standard for celebrities from the other side of the hemisphere. They're conditioned to behave as if every moment were an interview, unable to engage in genuine interaction. Don't let the fake take you off your pivot. Celebrities are a synecdoche for society. Blimey, who said that? Tom asked. Me. Pause. It's important to engage with public figures because they reflect *where we're at*. Where are we at? Everyone turned to me. *Scene City*, baby. Privileged immunity and ineffectuality. Same shit, different decade.

The next morning involved flying out into the thicket of it for the Cannes Film Festival. Thus ensued a week-long pause from the completely fictional London-based social events recounted in what to all intents and purposes is a novel. What began as a series of bullet points on my Notes app has become something else. People have started to notice my note-taking but they trust my discretion. Still, only a serious artistic endeavour, such as writing a novel, could justify spilling everyone's secrets. That's something the creative world would understand, and it would save me from ostracism. She isn't a gossip, she's a *novelist*, who will write an opus so magnum. No time. Ran to London City Airport, grabbed a flat white in my Burberry trench coat (gifted), and arrived at the boarding gate just on time — a meme of myself and a hip-swinging, heel-limping advertisement for the city. During my childhood, whenever we used to fly to the Middle East, we would be greeted in arrivals by family members, carrying balloons and bouquets of flowers. Nothing like that anymore. Just a stern-faced driver with my name misspelt on A4 paper. A demure moon peeked behind the acrylic of the aeroplane window. Still more words will mark these white pages upon my return, with the same fingerprints an artist leaves on clay. What's next? A fashionably late prologue, since the flight to Cannes marked my decision to seriously begin writing a novel.

MIDLOGUE

I am quite certain that I lived at the Tate.
Wittgenstein's Mistress, David Markson

There are always openings, if you can find them.
Lost in the Funhouse, John Barth

The homogenisation of the commercial art world appeals to imposters because it helps us forget our origins. To remember, I had to go back to where I came from, and write. That, right there, is apparently a novel-esque opening line, edited from an AI prompt on ChatLGBT. It was mid, even with my edits, hence its being shifted to the midlogue. I haven't emigrated, at least not since childhood.I grew up torrenting films on my laptop, so it makes sense to write this belated prologue at Cannes Film Festival. Why am I there? Hosting a Q&A with an actress I met in the bathrooms of Elgin House. She called me Gen Z Pauline Kael. Pauline Kale? Skimmed my

Notes app and was able to discern a plot. The plot: A group of young people in London's commercial art world lose the plot, and they only do it for the plot, falling together as if into themselves. Or: a landscape study of the social vacuum around artwork, observing a lifestyle which drifts across the city in a River Thames of parties.

Struggling against sleep, the urge to stop partying and start writing feels like the slap of a wet towel against cold tiles, a peristalsis of clarity that sharpens my way out with pencil lead. It will be fiction, because everyone I know is a character. Reality comes on fast and so does the urge to write a book for living people. The self has no containment in a situation as extreme as the city. Instead it multiplies into a scene, which disintegrates throughout the metropole. The only useful thing for us to do is to abandon the self and lean into the spectacle. We leak our multitudes into each other, spewing small talk with somebodyies at parties every night, awaiting the birth of futures that have already been repeated tirelessly in the past and will tirelessly repeat again. This is the fate of my generation, living as deep fakes of reality. Yet, the best stories are the ones that have been told about humanity since ancient times. What's interesting is figuring out new ways of telling them, devising languages and forms that reflect the cultural conditions of our time.

Before Chapter One, there was a backstory, this backstory: I was commissioned to write an essay for a book accompanying a YBA exhibition at a museum in Seoul. The YBA archives became minced meat in my hands, and spiced between fingers which still bear the pudginess of childhood.

The only way to really understand the YBAs was to be led astray. This involved inviting a group of friends to join me on a scholarly research trip to ye olde YBA party haunt, where they used to go at it hard and fast. The result? That Chapter One up there. See, our revelry always had some sliver of meaning, even before the beginning. But one art history essay can accommodate only so much partying. The essay had to turn into something long-form to warrant all the indulgence, which didn't stop after Chapter One, even after the essay was published. Hence, a novel. My avid notetaking eventually became a way to justify our nonstop partying. The YBAs had nearly been forgotten. Teddy christened our gaggle of gays the Young British Fags (YBFs) and duly renamed our group chat. It was an ironic nod to art history's insufferable nostalgia for cashed-out subcultures. This obsession breeds an inability to see anything new outside the prism of the past. AI is the culmination of our current inability to imagine a collective future. Chat, is this real? History is a nightmare from which young people are trying to awake, somewhere over the rainbow and under the starry plough.

The narrator-protagonist of *Scene City* is a twenty-three-year-old hedonist with a Notes app. She was born on 1 April 1999, the year the shit was meant to hit the fan, according to Nostradamus. Upon first entering her new world, she made constant efforts to betray her race and class, but soon dropped that act. You see, our young protagonist is trying to figure out how to most gracefully develop her own identity, in her new world. Her group of friends are older. They were born before Google was invented. We all form a village in Shoreditch, and there is a quantum of wantonness bred into all of us. The dreams of emerging artists, dealers, and critics dangle like wisps of hair before her eyes. Her eyes, her large, wide eyes of eternal brightness! Truman Capote had his swans of Fifth Avenue, and our narrator-protagonist has her pigeons of Liverpool Street Station. Her friendship group was already too deep within the establishment to be its prey. They had no desire to formalise themselves into a studio or collective, deterring the institutional culture vultures who would descend with public programming invitations at miscellaneous Kunsthalles. The art world commercialises social life through the commodification of identity, collectives, and community, desperate to access worlds beyond its own centre. Our lives move rapidly, as if hurrying towards the definitive end. In successive parties, our characters breathe between tenses and abandon time, caught up by city nights, stumbling into each other. The past in the present tense, a perfect sharpness that was not present during the prismatic moment of things happening. Time will always be disorienting; a condition of growing up in the diaspora and between time zones.

For a short while, attending an assembly line of parties was more interesting than writing about them. But now there is an umbilical cord attached to the novel. The essay was written, in the end, but this bastardised novel forced itself out, too. James Joyce is the baby daddy. Conceived via metempsychosis: the Word became flesh. Scheherazade in drag, but instead of writing a novel in a thousand and one nights, *Scene City* will be drafted next month, across four days and three nights, breakfast included, using the ideas and vignettes on my Notes app. Four days and three nights last as long as the art calendar's most important fair, which occurs in June, the cruellest month, compared to the darling buds of May. Shakespeare said every fair from fair sometime declines. The same goes for flying from art fair to art fair. Last year there were more pre-selling attempts with flashy PDFs, but fewer actual pre-sales, and some scrambling by collectors to free up capital on account of growing economic uncertainty . . . Certain political topics are avoided in the commercial art world, the same way Parisian women never mention going to the gym. Gallerists sometimes signal a tepid political engagement online, but this limp gesture doesn't extend beyond social media. Mind the gap between existence and resistance.

Scene City conjures the sensations of shared experiences in London through one authorial voice, a narrator-protagonist, this one, irreverent and rough with words. She will feel plural, the exact type of person the city tends to breed today. She will begin her novel by struggling to find herself in the decadence of the commercial art world, but encountering everyone else in the process. She'll feel overwhelmed. Does the process know she's trusting it? Front camera is the new auto-fiction, and other people's business interests her far more then her own. Since much of the novelistic research is unpublishable, many facts have been necessarily fictionalised, or maybe they haven't. I am not making myself up. Her narrative voice will be decentred. There will be no embarrassing use of the pronoun 'I' in the novel, only a yapping of consciousness in a stream of piss from party to party, released after the slog of a long workday. Not a stream of consciousness, but a stream of conscious observation. Abandoning my 'I' in favour of my eye. Shy like Tristram Shandy, the protagonist will be hesitant to burden you with her life story, or to begin from the beginning, *ab ovo et initio*. This authorial voice prefers to maintain the cool distance of a marginalised flâneuse.

Things fall apart; the centre cannot hold, and neither can 'I' after a few drinks. A first-person narrator has become generic, a trope of main-character syndrome. Our epoch is definable by an urge to document our own experiences obsessively, and my attempt at a novel is no different. We storify our lives and create narratives, anxiously giving the illusion that we have some grasp on or control over a world becoming increasingly uninhabitable. Reason has lost its political value. So has proof. Everything is fiction. Tidying our desks, exiting old browser tabs, and opening new reed scent diffusers. Gossip is a narrative device and taking drunken note of observations is an analytical tool, which will perhaps reveal some sort of truth. The Great Perhaps, the last words of Rabelais, the original proser. Even fiction—like this novel, at least—has become fictionalised non-fiction, minding the gap of neither medium. My generation is obsessed with narrativising its own lore, a chronically online illness of an era where people are only becoming more of the same. Thinking in captions, a software update of *Vile Bodies*, which was one of the first novels to include telephone conversations. Everything feels like nothing, an echo chamber perfectly embodied within the increasingly vacuous sociality of the art world, for those who are in it without a divine purpose.

The novel's milieu—London's commercial art world—is obsessed with culture but has not produced its own since the late 1900s. To criticise the commercial art world is easy, but few young people nowadays are willing to reimagine it completely. Those who don't reproduce the established ways of doing things become stuck in the rejection stage, endlessly critiquing what we call institutional critique, a self-referential discourse for those too scared to move on to the more difficult thing. Redemption is found in rebuilding: the excitement of quitting, figuring things out, and starting again, an impossible task always worth the effort. Being ethnically Middle Eastern, this is something like second nature to my *other* community and their relentless rebuilding of infrastructure after wars and colonial invasions. Being Arab is the coolest thing in the world. Sometimes you need to be surrounded by uncool people to be reminded of who you are. The artists around Romy are those most concerned with interrogating the relationship between the global elite and the rest of the world, but even then, the attainment of financial stability can be the strongest inducement to amnesia. In fact, artists are encouraged to be outsiders, which serves them well in this current zeitgeist of identity politics, as long as they hold a postgraduate degree from the Slade.

In 1970, Helio Oiticica wrote: I am not representing Brazil, or representing anything else, the ideas of representing and representation are over. Sadly not.

For all its whispering, there is no gossip in *Scene City*, unlike the old art-world columns from a museum called the Rotten Apple, which has developed a habit of jerking off to its own history. Whilst evoking something of a global village, the novel is set in Europe. This is where the upper echelons of society flocking to the art world tend to favour discretion, politeness, and chicness, above all else. Discretion is good taste and even better business. Besides, if my authorial voice slid too much of herself into the narrator, and unwittingly spilled someone's shrouded secret, no-one in the art world would care about the scandal, only about the fact of its being revealed. People are exactly what they choose to present to the world. In the art world, they are perfectly curated, and any invitation to 'go deeper' is calculated with the knowledge that anything shared would likely spread. The place where my voice comes from is a secret.

Our initial YBF research trip rolled senselessly into abundant nights and one long party in a tirelessly ongoing repetition of humanity. Thighs were slapped, heads were thrown back, shoulders were pushed forward, elbows retreated into ribs, and laughter burst from chests to open mouths. The nights grew longer and the days became tired and restless of having to be tied down to the week. The YBFs loved the idea of being main characters in a novel. They wanted to be infamous. Too bad. No fully fleshed-out characters here. Traditions of character and plot are for the next novel.

Everyone told me to keep *Scene City* short for their attention spans. This economic decision felt wise on account of our upcoming recession. A skinny novel is chic, Teddy said. People should have time to read this novel and none of us have any. Something was made of the nothing of the time in the short, quippy columns of Maeve Brennan's New York, the *crónicas* of Clarice Lispector's Rio de Janeiro and the sharp prose of Eve Babitz's Hollywood. *Scene City* will always tug on the question of when we'll stop partying, whilst the sole imperative is to keep going. The novel pieces together memories, fictionalising meaning out of the nothingness. The result is an ontological clawing, a fable of froth, and something like a pandemic of the ego, with too many similes in succession. Writing a serious thing like a novel eases the anxiety and existential nausea of partying. The main lesson a party girl can give about writing is how to steal lines. This skill involves connecting nothing with nothing, a line plucked from T. S. Eliot, who believed he was something.

Remembering is easier with accomplices: Notes app and Getty Images, which can also be used to give a fictional logic and chronology to events. My generation are too overstimulated to remember anything without assistance, creating a numbness that makes holding on to memories difficult—recollection further stunted by nightly drinking. We have more exposure to information than ever before but we're becoming dumber and lazier. Our brains are only able to retain soundbites. Yap-yap core. In *La Préparation du roman*, Roland Barthes wrote that note-taking gave him a form of security. Retaining memories is a practice that resists morning-after amnesia, when the night feels too far away and all that remains is a world-ache wiping the forehead from forenoon to afternoon. The pointlessness of everything is exacerbated by the gig economy and its concept of the freelance, which is excruciatingly unstructured. One historical equivalent of being a creative freelance in London is the dandy, the type written about by Charles Baudelaire and lived by Oscar Wilde. There is little more existentialist than existing outside office life and being forced to invent other options within our relative freedoms. We can do anything, technically. But somehow it only ever amounts to reformer Pilates on a Wednesday afternoon. We could live radically otherwise, but no-one thinks about that. The days flow into each other, without a god or full-time boss. So, we run through London, chew a mouthful of it, and spit it out like a wad of gum. How can we turn this into an experiment in living? How much of our time is our own? How can we use our freedom to build a slightly freer life under capitalism unlike anyone before us? Is this what the creative freelance class discusses each night on Arnold Circus stools over buzzy, delectable orange wine?

The city has a long history of translating debauchery and reckless partying into cultural movements. The Bright Young Things, the Decadent poets, YBAs, etc. Average faces illuminated by candlelight have always become extraordinary. These groups were unscathed by any sort of serious historical misfortune and were likely oblivious at the time to the changes they effected in the social order. There is little difference between the social activities which occurred then and ours now. The scene stays, only the faces change. Champagne Cynics, Vaping Visionaries, Digital Dadas. The British Ruins has a nice ring to it. Each historical movement comes with the side order of a new literary style. She was positively a harlot in scarlet, feather plumb and feet numb from those steep heels that are all the rage now—and so on. The glitter, noise, and bored young faces remain, becoming hard and intelligent when necessary. There are other timeless characteristics of the city: the rain begins with a drizzle, as if trying not to fall. Some images in inner-city novels persist, such as blistering asphalt and wetted ashes, from Sam Selvon to John Dos Passos, who taught us about cities and the wafts of wet bricks that built the pavements before tarmac. There is rarely any grasp of where we are going in the moment, but history dictates that we must go somewhere, and novels are handy in that regard. Their cities are our cities, which continued to grow without them, even though each epoch was convinced they were bigger and brighter. Today, there is a new fear greater than the anxiety that nothing will happen: our waiting for the world to end. Finally, it seems we have caught up with the city, and we're facing each other for the last time.

6

My return from Cannes Film Festival involved a summons for the second coming of the Harpo Club, a legendary members' club in Soho. The Harpo is a numinous descendant of the Gargoyle Club, which was on Dean Street, and of the same ilk as Wheeler's and the Colony Room. The Harpo is down the road from Quo Vadis, which was a brothel at one time and home to Karl Marx at another. They do a good smoked eel sandwich. The Harpo was formerly haunted by the YBAs and was recently purchased by the hospitality arm of an art gallery. It's called buying history. They wanted to resurrect the vibe that once made it the hottest place in town. All of the party girls were invited to the resurrection. There were other types of guest: those who made art and those who made money, and sometimes a happy third, the art world bisexual who can do both. Joan Didion wrote that great hotels are social ideas, and the same can be said for members' clubs. Building a new club from scratch in today's economy has become difficult, because its exclusivity stifles the membership revenue demanded by investors. There seems to be more business potential in reviving historical clubs with existing histories. The McDonald's of these clubs, which shall not be named, deactivated my membership because we jumped naked in the pool after midnight. The manager screamed at me ballistically. It was so cringe. The ban didn't bother me at all. No-one interesting goes there anymore.

The young professionals in London's creative industries are partying at a new members' club called the Sixty-Nine, off Grosvenor Square. It's dark and cosy and maximalist, with Morris & Co. wallpaper. On the night of the grand opening, a cute girl was hanging outside. Invited her in as my plus one. She grabbed my elbow and squealed. Is that Leonardo DiCaprio? The host rolled his eyes and walked off. We were air-kissed by a Somali supermodel, the face that launched a thousand trips to Alaïa. The usher ushered in Usher, who brought a rapper, offset with a bottle of Bacardi. If he speaks to you, don't say you recognise him. Just talk to him like he's a normal person. She nodded. Spotted her later that night saying something about Alan Smithee, a famous director, but using only his first name, implying that she knew him. The person she was speaking to, an indie rockstar who actually knew him, asked how they met. She glanced at me. She is interning at Dérosian, Alan Smithee is her boss's client. Goalie save. The cute girl glazed on lip gloss and her eyes went blank. Excellent. Slipped home. The party wasn't for me. Which was fine. Not everything should be for everyone, despite what we've fooled ourselves into believing. Where did you go? the cute girl texted me the next morning. She had gone home with the rockstar. She's a rock chick, and she likes to rock out. Now they're married, and she's pregnant with their child.

In Kensington, another members' club recently reopened with a riad-style garden and a fake James Turrell artwork. Tom came with me to the opening. There was a private concert in the garden which lasted about an hour. The famous rapper didn't break his gangster routine in front of the chinless millennials jumping up and down in their pale blue shirts, punching the air with cigarettes and glasses of champagne. White dancing is moving to lyrics instead of the beat. We ate dinner beforehand at a nearby Iraqi restaurant, one of the many named Masgouf. My Prada kid gloves clutched a takeaway bag containing plastic containers of leftovers, which a British romcom titan said was 'very charming'. Tom saw a few of his friends, such as a ghostwriter with peach hair and wolfish itch, and a bro-ish DJ who designed a limited series of football scarves. They weren't gay, they were studio mates. The first thing the DJ asked me: How is Caleb? In my novel, he is the boyfriend-of. Romy is devastatingly monogamous, Tom sighed. So chic, the DJ replied. Monogamy. So out, it's in. Fidelity is the modern version of having faith. Being a football fan, you probably wouldn't be cut out for it. Ha, why not? Because football is for men who enjoy the experience of wildly fluctuating emotions within a short time frame. He laughed across the skyline. Barf. Either way, you shouldn't trust her, Tom added. She's too verbal. She doesn't do drugs. And those big eyes are dangerous. They see too much. My big eyes were already busy watching an A24 executive snogging a twenty-four-year-old. Nearby, Courteney Cox or Demi Moore held cold champagne on her forehead to cool down. Tom, have you read *The Coldest Winter Ever* by Sister Souljah? Tom pointed to the bar, look, an MTA 2.0. Model-turned-actress? No, that's MTA 1.0. The latest model is model-turned-activist. Well, she has fantastic zygomatics. Is that Amal Clooney and her husband? Cigarettes lit over muffled cool noises. If you're so smart, then why are you sleeping alone?

Sorry, so many unnecessary deets. Landed back in London after moonset and just before sunrise. Spent my morning in front of an analogue camera, posing for Mehdi. He photographed me for the upcoming issue of a Paris fashion magazine, whose offices are near the Mirabeau bridge of Apollinaire's greatest love poem. Langston and Mehdi's home decor is quietly opulent, a felicity of billowy swansdown laid on springer rushes with canopies of goat pelt. It is full of farmhouse features, griffin-footed furniture, and mid-century modern paraphernalia. Their home is homely, unlike those of many young people in the city, whose apartments just feel like somewhere to sleep. How was Cannes? Mehdi asked. A bunch of ageing filmmakers asking about my favourite streamer, because that's what some model-skater told them was the future. Most of us agree that the future of culture is not AI, at least. AI can only regurgitate pre-existing information. So, it's not the future, or even the present, it's the past. The future of culture is worldbuilding. Creating an immersive infrastructure and an alternative future that people want to move into and join, since every other possibility we're being offered is looking bleak. Plus, everyone wants to feel like they're on a real journey. Langston and Mehdi's home attracts glamorous women to their sofa, where qualms are divulged more freely than over cocktails at Elgin House. It was early in the morning, but an Italian socialite was already lying sideways on their sofa discussing her favourite abortion. She decided it was the one in Gstaad. They had pinhole lights on the ceiling of the clinic that looked like stars. (So does the women's sauna in Claridge's.) Semen stains Alpine summits from the spermarium to the crematorium. There are certain things women shouldn't pay for, like abortions or drinks. The woman was of Medici lineage. Caleb once fucked me in the rose bushes of the Villa Medici at night, and then we stumbled naked through the garden after hearing the bark of the security guard's dog. Hit my nose with the stem of a rose, like John Giorno.

We listened to the socialite's soliloquy over a pot of freshly brewed morning coffee. It is considered socially acceptable to make conversation about intellectual topics in the art world, but people are rarely prepared to talk about their private lives. Unless, of course, everyone is inebriated or you're a socialite and being messy is your shtick. Sybille Bedford novels taught me the difference between bourgeoisie and aristocracy. It is easier to talk about your favourite painter *du jour*. The problem is that many people apply this surface-level relationship logic to their romantic partners and become frustrated when a deeper emotional connection does not evolve. Many couples in the art world make too much aesthetic sense; without any chemistry. The heart is a child that cannot hide the truth. You can clearly tell when people *are* fucking. It's usually with a person they're not supposed to be fucking. Shared an example with Langston. Noooo. How do you know they're fucking?! He gave her a solo booth at the fair. How was the fair? Idk, ask Tom. Tom said: *We're very happy*. That's the phrase gallerists use when they don't want to talk about money. Anyway. The fissure of entry into other emotional lives rarely opens, from fear of appearing unprofessional. Andy Warhol said that there's nothing more bourgeois than being afraid of being bourgeois. Seasonal flowers that fester smell worse than weeds.

Mehdi walked briskly to Kensington Memorial Park with me scurrying behind him in an Alaïa body suit and knee-high boots. The cover girl of cultural criticism. A make-up artist cleaned me up as clean as a broom cleans. It was unbearably cringe to wear a night look on a Tuesday morning. Fathers walking their greyhounds in the park observed me with bemused expressions. A serious art critic appeared with her young son, who gawked at me with a Chupa Chups in her open mouth. What do you say, kid? Goated. Mehdi bought me a bubble-gum-flavoured ice-cream to sit and eat on the side of the pavement. It wasn't Gelupo, but it would do. The clouds raced across the sky.

It is a skill to dress for the full day, requiring fastidious layering. This is crucial for art fairs. Wrapping up is essential for the early museum breakfast, as are comfy shoes for the actual fair, and then everything can be peeled off to reveal an outfit suitable for an austere gallery dinner and a subsequent party. Art fairs are essentially just really fancy car boot sales. At one last year, Tom fished a Dior x Peter Doig jumper from a bin where a collector had thrown it. Art people are more fashionable than fashion people. Fashion people these days try too hard to seem intellectual, a Graydon Carter wannabe once whispered into my ear. Beyond. Dressing in the art industry is less about following trends and more about establishing loyalty to certain brands, particularly those led by creative directors who are art adjacent. The art world often resists fashion when it is too explicitly about product. Some creative directors plonk a different painter on their jumpers each season. Others collect specific artists over a long period of time for their personal collections. We wrapped up the shoot. A neighbourhood cat rubbed up against my bare legs in a cheap romance.

Langston and Mehdi invited me to join them for lunch in Vauxhall. Not wanting to waste the shoot makeup was enough reason to go out. We crossed the river on the bridge of our noses. The restaurant was on the riverbank where the water lay dead. And there he was—Large Benjamin, his silly clock face overlooking the Thames. Sweet Thames, run softly, till my novel ends. The restaurant sits within the tradition of Lyle's, Brat, and Bistrotheque. They serve delicious seasonal cuisine. The old-school spot for grouse is Rules. The artefacts of carcasses are tossed in an overflowing tip. Information is best digested by eating.

The culinary blueprints for London's modern food scene are St John and Rochelle Canteen. They are London stalwarts run respectively by husband and wife, who also bear association to the YBAs. St John is from the lineage of Sweeting's, a seafood restaurant which has served the dimpled fins of John Dory since the year 1830. The nymphs are now departed. Consider the lobster. Other restaurants in the same milieu as Sweeting's are caught in the ebb and flow of Soho. Beside Bentley's Oyster Bar and Grill used to be Sibylla's, which was *the* nightclub of Swinging London. Aristocracy made way for meritocracy. Suddenly the cool kids weren't necessarily rich but necessarily stylish. Working-class artists with swag swung to the summit of the social strata. They existed within a scene, too, but that's someone else's novel. Or better yet, a film. Except there are already tons of London 'groupie' films. My favourites are Nicolas Roeg's *Performance* and Lindsay Shonteff's *Permissive*. Do groupies still exist?

During my late teens, many trendy parties happened at a hotel halfway along Shoreditch High Street. The people in attendance were over-invited, over-accepting and over-exposed, a classic case of clout clot. The hotel shut down when the owner hanged himself in the penthouse. The Normal Hotel, which is very normal, opened in King's Cross. That became the new hotel party spot. The doors of a corridor lined up like dominos. My favourite hotel room activities include watching foreign game shows, ordering Chinese takeaways, and sharing riddles. Speaking of which, last Sunday, Samira pointed out to me a man at the Normal bar giving another man—one with a wedding ring—the keys to his room. It was so the married man could hook up with a Swedish girl he'd just met. If you let a man shenan once, he will shenanigan. Once the illicit couple left, we asked a drunk man about the scene. Were they together last Sunday? Never in a month of Sundays. He knew the married man. He said it was simply a gesture of solidarity for the sex acts of star-crossed lovers, and for women with battle-swollen breasts and areolas the greyish pink of uncooked prawns. Right. And apparently her insignificant other beat her. If you can't change the man, change man.

There are other new hotels in London now, most of them gold-edged and tackily decorated for the wealthy transplants and their long stays. Teddy and Arabella West hosted an art fair party at yet another new hotel chain addition to Soho. The bathroom drains exploded, and sewage seeped all over the dance floor. That didn't stop anyone. The girls with nice shoes were hoisted onto boys with strong shoulders. Dilara Findikoglu hosted a Halloween Ball there, too. Arabella West just opened an eponymous gallery in Wolfgang Tillman's old studio. There is a local phenomenon of fabulous West London–bred women like Arabella with long gothic dyed-black hair, in the same style as the protagonist in Frances Newman's novel *The Hard-Boiled Virgin* or legendary party host Helena Kallianiotes of Los Angeles. This phenomenon is a slightly cooler alternative to the blonde and bird-like prima gallerinas, the type who graduate from lacrosse captain to tragically uncool art history graduate, with a desperation to be liked by — Romy!

Tom interrupted from the margins. Don't be a bitch. What happened to women supporting women? It's Pride Month, Tom. Save it for International Women's Day. Most of the girlies working in galleries come from wealth. They don't get paid much. And even though the directors can earn a pretty penny if they get commission, the work is still being sold to billionaires. That's like most industries, but in the art world, the close proximity is unnerving. You don't work in a sweatshop in China and have Mr Kering in the office next to you.

The Harpo Club's resurrection was as outrageously baroque as could be imagined by the Swiss diocese of the Baumer & Baumann gallery. Galleries tend to have open relationships with their members' clubs and bed-hop between venues. A favourite seems to be the Union Club, a veritable Greek Street institution thanks to its tiny burgers and lack of pretension. The renaissance of members' clubs saves us from endless nights in a basement on Shaftesbury Avenue that feels like a sex dungeon, not that this narrator would know anything about that. Upon our arrival at the Harpo, chefs were assembled in a corner cracking open thousands of oysters. Other corners housed towers of lobster, asparagus, or champagne coupes. There were collectors sat in the dark, waiting for someone to do something amusing. The constant pythonic stare of a thin-lipped man with pupils tinctured by Percy Pigs stung me from across the bar. He was staring cock-eyed at my tits. Something to do with shipping, Keshav whispered. Has anyone written about the neocolonialism of offshore logic? Intersectional imperialism, anyone? He's one of those collectors who started buying contemporary art decades ago because the artists were his friends, Keshav continued. Then he built a house in St Moritz and tapped out. St Moritz is the Miami of Switzerland. The receding shoreline of his hairline was once a rough tide of sandy waves. The man walked over and inquired his body towards me, smelling like shame and Maison Margiela Replica. His cluttered gutter of snot was hooked and pointed upright.

A legendary painter sat at the bar, a woman who looked like Patti Smith, her fringe a blindfold. Always respect older women, your elderflowers. The woman signalled with an index finger for me to join her. In a broken accent she said my face bore a resemblance to the young Hanna Schygulla, a favourite actress of Fassbinder's. It's not true, but she talked and talked until her words replaced and killed her feelings. Get this: a novelist who wants to disappear and who thinks people communicate much better without words. Illiterate yourself in these drunken nights. There was something relatable about her. Then again, painters and novelists are always getting mixed up in my head. Marlene Dumas and Marguerite Dumas. Takashi Murakami and Haruki Murakami. The woman pulled up an image of another actress, Maria Schneider from Bernardo Bertolucci's *Last Tango in Paris*, a soubrette with a poster smile. She insisted that the resemblance was uncanny, she who wrests old images, with horniness flung on an empty canvas. Elderly people are gangsters of justification with their you-remind-me-of-someone-from-my-past lines. Looking like someone who wasn't myself and without anything else left to say, her easy fantasy left the room.

My friends yelped on the other side of the room and emptied baggies from Le Cagole handbags onto the mid-century oak tables. A Balenciaga model too ugly not to be beautiful led the conversation. They had garnered controversy for tattooing their hairless cat. Samira was great craic and plunged nose-first onto the table like an Olympian. *Scene City*? More like *Snow City*. She slipped a bunch of asparagus into her bag, but a waiter caught her and she had to put it back. Keshav started pandemonium in Londinium because the lobster rolls ran out. At the beginning of this sentence, he hadn't kissed anyone, so he kissed Oscar, then Samira, then Tom, so by the end of the sentence, he had kissed three people. Tom had to run off to a party meeting. From party to partisan. What party? Samira asked, sipping on her skinny bitch (vodka and soda). A political party. Ok, guerrilla. Did you just call me a gorilla? There was no other way to survive the mayhem than to drink an Irish amount of alcohol. Oscar dropped a napkin, and a collector quickly pocketed it as a souvenir, since we started a drunken rumour he was a rising art star, and now the rumour is becoming true, with the market being so speculative and all. They sparred. Oscar was spared by Keshav. His heart erected. A Pynchon-esque hard-on reflex. A semi of semi-consciousness. Would you like to put your hand in my pocket? Keshav and Oscar made out for the eighth time this year. Our Achilles and Patroclus. Their mouths moulded kisses.

The party hosts, Baumer & Baumann, are evolving into

a lifestyle brand. They have a farmhouse in Somerset. The month prior, we all took an early train there to attend an opening. All except Keshav, whose baby sister was in town and wanted to go people watching at Allpress Dalston. The train steward who wheeled the coffee cart unknowingly skewered us when he asked: Why does everyone want oat milk in their coffee today? Each train carriage contained art world tables. Just like the early-morning Eurostar journey between London and Paris, between two big art fairs. Everyone gazed out the misty window at the same Elsworth Kelly *Train Landscape* painting. Art fairs are like normal life in triple time. Instead of one dinner or one opening each night, there are at least three of each. It is good to keep a diary in order to stay grounded. Otherwise the days take off and you take flight and you behave like a nimbuscile, cradled by the clouds. These are the most difficult days to keep steady, when you are living too fast to write any of it down. Samira held forth about the recent city-wide bed bug panic in Paris, which she falsely believed was a hoax perpetrated by the publicists of the London art fair. Someone told me that going to an art fair in the Grand Palais feels like being inside a Ladurée macaron box. The glass ceiling is currently being renovated. The London art fair takes place in a tent. It's owned by the fair's founder, whose uncle was a park ranger. London-based gallerists try vainly to get American collectors to stop off in London first, but unfortunately their wives prefer shopping in Paris.

The most agreeable thing about art parties in London

is their quiet volume. Everyone's voice is low. Our severity of manners gives the seductive illusion of classy restraint. Speak in cursive font, please. Andy Warhol had a quiet rasp, which is why he was shot in a city of such unbearably loud people. Hypothetically, in the unlikely event a wild night out should land me in a beauty pageant, my answer to any question about world peace would be to suggest speaking at a low volume. The world would be a better place. WWIII *who*? Caleb gets annoyed at my whispering, but he's all talk. Whispering into an ear is so intimate. In a crowded party you can feel more present by engaging someone in a quiet conversation, the type of tête-à-tête where nothing else in the room exists. Baumer & Baumann gallerinas have mortgage accents—posh, husky, and low voices—that are indigenous to upscale West London. Born with a silver knife in their mouths, spewing words that dazzle the skulls of baby lambs and sentences that create embroideries of mythologies. Those beautiful nymphs ensnare men with their family homes in Ogygia. There are many brilliantly archaic nouns used in the echelons of the upper class, like gimlet, said in a raspy tone. My tone is more sharp-edged, cutting like a credit card.

The night became restless, and we abandoned conversation for the dance floor. Pimped by death, possessed in the shadows. Teddy twirled flamboyantly with the freedom of a meaningless gesture in a world of meaningless gestures. Samira hastened to the bar to restock our hands with drinks. Get me one of those piranha cocktails. What? The ones they do in Brazil. Don't you mean a caipirinha? Sure, a caipirinha. Alright, *um* caipirinha on the way. Gracias, bitch. You mean *obrigado*. Huh? Never mind. Teddy spun on the dance floor and fell over. Ow! The art world doesn't dance but my group of friends dance any time we get the chance. The DJ at the Harpo Club was as old as a towering sequoia, opening his mouth with a wrinkling bark. He must've been born in the early '90s or something. He was soon joined by a young DJ who had a Patreon for track IDs. My soul swayed easily on the dance floor while the DJ tunescrolled. Samira laughed with a daub of sugary flour stuck to her cheek and whipped her long black hair like gypsy women in that traditional Iraqi dance. Sometimes after work we meet at the Old Blue Last and jump up and down to Kate Bush until we get tired, flapping with life like Lucia Joyce and fatigued at the corners of our hard-boiled eyes. Against snobbish opinion it is possible to enjoy an evening out in Shoreditch if you just shift your perspective. The fresh puke left on my doorstep by a hen party the night before can easily be mistaken for a splatter of bird food. Broken glass on the street? An ode to Yoko Ono's 1965 performance *Morning Piece*. The night she sold glass shards in Tokyo labelled with the date and time of a future morning. The tarmac grit crystals of broken glass shards. Learning how to fabricate meaning in a city is a skill, and we are low-life professionals. O O O O that modernist rag.

7

A nasty hangover seared my forehead, but the fridge contained only champagne and a few half-eaten chunks of cheese that an Italian gallery sent us for Christmas. Beats Babybels or Cheesestrings. We have an American fridge. My mum always wanted an American fridge. America, the land of innovation, where water bottles have plastic caps that come off, without flapping at the mouth. Thousands drink the nectar from a flower the Euphrates has nourished with dew. Breakfast is always such a headache. *The bundle of accident and incoherence that sits down for breakfast.* Me by W. B. Yeats. Disillusionment entered the chat but there was no time, with me being late for a meeting in Chelsea. My feet hadn't landed that way since my bildungsroman era—now, you're reading a *Künstlerroman*, btw—at a modelling agency just off the King's Road. The other girls took the fashion world by storm, while it became clearer to me why storms are named after people. The punk icon,

Jordan, from Vivienne Westwood's Sex shop at 430 King's Road, starred in some fantastic films; *Nightshift* is the most underrated. People used to give her hell. Hell is a city much like London, wrote Percy Bysshe Shelley, assumably referring to the ridiculous amount of time it takes to get from one side of the city to the other. Hell pays for heaven. Gorgi Gallery is located on the King's Road. It was my first voluntary or non-school-trip-related visit to a museum, to see the Chanel exhibition with a friend. The gallery is old-school legendary in the art world, founded by Michael Gorgi, who is Arab, surprisingly.

My Arab family are more Barnet than Chelsea. We're the type that keeps our sofas wrapped in plastic. Spending time with my family as an adult helped me understand what community meant, which is different from the phoney way it gets thrown around by pseudo-academics in creative classes. Community-building? Bitch, please. There are certain things uniting Arabs across classes, like growing up knowing Israel is a killing machine more than a gay beach resort. Our inheritance of memories is haunted by the gaping mouths of machine guns. (Romy, the closest to a bullet you've ever gotten is a nutribullet, Samira texted.) Edgware Road is in the throes of redevelopment, although there are still uncles smoking shisha in cafés throughout the day. Once, while sat in my favourite café on Edgware Road, the one run by Iraqi women and covered in artificial flowers, a cuckold stormed inside and approached his wife with a knife. He opened his mouth to hell, and she howled into it. In one swift movement, the uncles in the corner playing backgammon jumped up and, with the athleticism of men half their age, pounced upon the man, pinned him to the floor, and started beating him. It took him a while to untangle himself and flee. The uncles strolled back to their tables and resumed their game. If this was a café for white people everyone would have screamed and hidden under the tables. All are damnable and damned, each one damning, damns the other.

King's Road is marked by a pimple called Sloane Square which was thronged on account of the annual Chelsea Flower Show. The Sloane Rangers are more pink-rose hand cream and Cartier Love bracelet than the socialites from Holland Park and Notting Hill. They're considered less cool, somehow. To an unaccustomed eye, however, they're all just rich white women with Coutts cards, deadly-slim reapers. Most of them are actually deeply insecure and feel superlatively malformed. Dropped into a café on Pavilion Road and asked for some water. What kind of water? Still water. What kind of still water would you like? Whatever you have. She startled me with a lengthy soliloquy on the different types of still water on their menu, from mineral to still to spring water, with various alkaline and purification levels. Voss, my overwhelmed voice interrupted her, Voss. As one goes to Lourdes on pilgrimage, my pilgrimage as a child was the Southern Railway train to Bond Street, and as one acquires Holy Water in Lourdes, my smaller hands would buy a single bottle of fancy purified water, complete with glorious yellow paper bag, in the Selfridge's food hall, with pocket money. Then a trip to the big Primark, to stock up on black plimsolls. The fancy purified water bottle would become a playground accessory, reused until the glass neck developed grime. It was placed, very visibly, on my desk with sushi from Tesco, and its coveted yellow paper bag. When the bag ripped, the bottle was carried in a Little Brown Bag, bought during a visit to my uncle in Dubai in the early noughts, before the influencers started going. Your Kylie Jenner is my Haifa Wehbe.

My meeting was in Café Baptiste, next to Sloane Square Station. It gives the impression of being an old-school institution but opened only a decade ago. Café Baptiste has the same owners as another fake historical restaurant in Green Park, which has become a veritable spot. Met with my PhD thesis supervisor of toneless voice and urbane manners. He was in town from ye olde institution. Luckily, my scholarship gave me permission to do the whole thing remotely. Wouldn't have survived it up there. During the meeting he dislodged a chia seed from between two yellow teeth using the point of a toothpick and proceeded to clean behind his nails with a fork. He gazed outside solemnly and muttered something about antiquity. Pimlico Road nearby is the destination for antique shops which—unlike Café Baptiste—have genuinely been around forever. A Christopher Gibbs–type owner of a local antique shop once told me stories about old Chelsea while we sat around a wooden table in his basement drinking filter coffee that flowed sideways into glazed ceramic cups. Eyebrows wiry as pubes and a snail trail of silver around his wrist called a bracelet . . . He will be in the novel, there. The area used to be populated by barrow boys who would store their wheelbarrows in garages and take them out for the markets, which are now posh playgrounds of lawn spawn. Back then, Pimlico Road was connected to the Thames via a wet tongue where people unloaded timber by horse and carriage. WET, says the Mowalola vest top all the girls are wearing. Throw a cigarette butt into grey and choppy Thames water. An offering to the gods! Barrow boys used to mix their milk with water for the sake of economy. We tend to the dead like roses.

Customers buying antiques today have less interest in historical value or uniqueness, but more in material, durability, and sustainability. Or at least, that's what antique dealers have told me. There was a time when antique dealers were forced to visit estate auctions far outside of London, but now everything is available to view on PDFs. You circle all the items you want, like a child before Christmas earmarking toys in an Argos catalogue. Looking at a PDF of artwork, instead of seeing it in real life, is like watching porn instead of having sex. Pre-sales make verifying the quality of china trickier, but experts can always judge the authenticity. It is easy to love these old London stories because they give you a history and make you feel a part of something, like those old '60s London films. Like *Billy Liar* (1963), *London in the Raw* (1964), *Darling* (1965), *The Pleasure Girls* (1965), *Tonite Let's All Make Love in London* (1967), *Bronco Bullfrog* (1969) . . . Following *Bronco Bullfrog*, the director released *Private Road* (1971), which starred Bruce Robinson, the guy who directed *Withnail and I*, as a debut novelist. The pigeons in London films are always far more domesticated and attractive than in reality. Like in *A Warm December*, where Sidney Poitier poses romantically in Trafalgar Square surrounded by fluffy and well-behaved Hollywood pigeons. Hollywood shows them sipping water from puddles rather than flying into your mouth in Paddington Station to steal a masticated chunk of sausage roll. Mangy pigeons who have never been cooed at. Pigeons in the olden days were better fed, now they're probably all coeliac. Romy? My thesis supervisor looked at me expectantly. Sorry, could you repeat your question?

My next meeting was at a fashion brand's offices, which looked like the Equinox gym in Tribeca. From Homi Bhabha's postcolonial book *Third Space* to Third Space gym; a spin-class Spinoza disassociating in downward dog. Wellness warriors are so focused on looking within they ignore everything happening outside of themselves. We've become so obsessed with wellness, and applaud self-indulgence, because in an era where we have so little power, having control over our bodies gives the illusion that we have control over our lives. My legs can now comfortably jog up the two steep flights of escalators to exit the Elizabeth Line at Liverpool Street Station. Up the airy mountain, down the rushy glen. Working out is fun but walking out is more fun because everyone dramatically exits the gym wearing hard clothes and real shoes, bound for a bank headquarters nearby. They are all ripped, side-stepping between spreadsheets and bedsheets. Samira once dated a man from my gym, although the only machine that impressed her was an ATM machine. It didn't last more than a few nights. He kept circling it around inside her, as if whisking custard for a cherry trifle. The gym bro regalia inspired me to buy a briefcase simply to take it to the gym, something to accessorise with a frown as if my stocks just fell, slipped down or something. The women wear delululemon and On Running trainers, carrying Stanley cups. Me too. Except my Stanley cup is filled with Coke Zero. Activewear has become the new streetwear. Caleb used to go to my gym but now he only stretches canvases. Gallerinas are often totally obsessed with health, or maybe they're just obsessed with being skinny. Women dressing their salads with Prada, their raw face-bones prominent above sunken cheeks, like high heels in grass. Here, bitch, eat a canapé. Classic gallerina debate: Lanserhof vs FX Mayr. Two Austrian health resorts which are practically the same. Lanserhof has a health club opposite a members' club in Mayfair, where you can watch *Shrek 2* while getting an MRI scan.

Health fads in the art world have always been as excessive as its substance abuse. Usually, it's a woman of substance. Andy Warhol drank carrot juice every morning no matter what went into his mouth the night before. Being fit after forty has become a bigger status symbol than a G-Wagon. Men turn forty and suddenly become obsessed with Japanese whisky, the *uisce beatha*. Japan for straight men is Ireland for weird women. There's a new play by Annie Baker set in a Lanserhof-esque establishment. Another buzzy playwright once joked on an airport shuttle that if a play was going to be set in an imaginary luxury health retreat, the cast should at least have been skinny. It's true: you see mostly skinny health freaks at luxury health retreats and expensive gyms. Once upon a time, a West London wellness influencer was standing near me at a party and my negroni mouth told her, without any prior introduction, that she was the reason there was a juicer in my kitchen. Beside her was a trad housewife who became famous for using a blowtorch on homemade desserts. A woman's place is on a man's face.

Western wellness capitalises on the fact that humans are never completely well. The result of a full body scan will never be perfect. So, they give you all these new vitamins to integrate into your routine, and then you become neurotic about it. St Pancreas over here—gestures to Samira—almost overdosed on vitamins. Feeling better has become prioritised over becoming better. Losing weight nowadays means becoming better at not being hungry. My food intolerances have transformed me into a fussy eater, although there are exceptions. Thesis: homemade ethnic food is inherently good for you. Arab food tastes better than skinny feels. Took a fashion editor from Paris for dolma at my favourite spot on Edgware Road after a JW Anderson runway show. The onion dolma are my favourite. Sometimes my brothers let me join in with noisily hitting the bottom of the dolma pan with a wooden spoon; the dolma is first flipped upside down upon a serving plate, with the oil-soaked bread on top. You know it's a good Arab restaurant when they give you the free lentil soup, fresh bread, and tea. No-one blinked an eye when they saw me enter in a gold silk gown and neck-high heels early on a Sunday morning.

Thinking of dolma made Vesuvius rumble, but it was a fashion brand office so the kitchen cupboards were empty. Or almost empty. My meeting took place on the kitchen counter over a giant bowl of Special K. Hungry, my stomach counselled me. Keshav texted the POC division of YBF and booked a dinner reservation at Rita's Dining. He named our WhatsApp group chat 'Foreigners Everywhere', the title of the upcoming Venice Biennale. Venice highlight? Keshav asked. The ink cuttlefish at Ristorante da Ivo. Someone give the national pavilion to Romy's man so she can be First Lady of the British Pavilion. Her outfits would slay. True. The biennale exhibitions often shy away from contemporary artists, especially those favoured by the global market, and tend towards grassroots or so-called outsider art. Global South–themed exhibitions are usually anthropological, meaning that the quality of the artwork often matters less to Western academic curators than issues pertaining to identity. We, Foreigners Everywhere, ate chicken pie and had soft-brain conversations. The best fish pie in London is from the old-school Irish restaurant in Mayfair, the one run by Michael Caine. Mouth is too full, can't remember name. We were in the company of an actual foreigner who was in town for his first UK solo exhibition. He was from Dakar but had just come from Marrakesh, where none of the high-end restaurants had let him inside. He was dressed in his usual paint-splattered clothes and not spruced up like all the other Black foreigners. Liberal Arab elites *love* posting infographics of Audre Lorde on Palestine but will never reckon with the rampant anti-Blackness amongst their own people.

People are less up-front racist in London, Samira explained. They're more . . . indifferent. Which has its own violence. But it's better. Romy doesn't have a problem because she's light-skinned and skinny. Samira shut up, you're literally built like a Pixar mom. Ya, Romy. Eh? Kol khara. Fuck you.

We groped through a tangle of hard bodies in the brittle noise of Oxford Street towards Softcore, a group exhibition opening at a gallery in Soho. The sourcing of interesting exhibition titles is the hunting and gathering of the modern world. Perhaps the actual group show is the friends we make along the way. Drank champagne from a paper cup and listened to gossip from recent social events, all of them worth missing. It was the usual crowd, seasoned with a funny-looking man wearing a ghastly patterned suit and fedora who couldn't have served even if he was drafted. He used to be a DJ, Keshav said. Now he's an Old Masters collector living in the Cotswolds. What happened? He contracted HIV from a dirty turntable needle at a rave. What was he doing to the needle? Fucking it? What happens in Canning Town stays in Canning Town. Most collectors don't go to busy openings, unless it is for a successful artist with a long waiting list. Then they go and schmooze the eponymous gallerist. Successful artists don't fantasise about growing waiting lists of collectors eager to buy their artwork. They usually aspire to the utopia of working alone without a studio team, as they did early in their careers. Rembrandt's students used to paint coins on the floor and laugh when he stooped to pick them up. It is difficult to manage a studio, especially when you're dealing with people who feel entitled to claim ownership over the work. Many studio assistants, particularly of my generation, believe in the abolition of hierarchy, which makes getting anything done difficult, and that's coupled with a moral policing of the artist and whatever they're working on, which must not offend any gaze. Some artists have to constantly tiptoe around their team, unable to ask anyone to research anything that may cause offence, until it becomes unclear who is actually working for whom. Artists used to be the people in society who could follow the dark twisted fantasies of their dream lives without being held accountable. Now it's the finance guys.

The after-party happened at a buzzy new Japanese bar in Soho. Each cocktail contained one large rectangular ice cube that looked like the ice cubes in the Joan Jonas video *Ice Drawing Sculpture*. There was Italian ham on a wooden board, too. It was Florine's last day working at the gallery, so we repeatedly clinked ice cubes to that. She drank many glasses of ice cubes. The chunk of her black heel hooked over a metal barstool was the only thing keeping her upright. She took a drink, and then the drink took her. Her left palm held her chin, as sandpaper elbows scratched the velvet counter. Tom passed me a time-sensitive tequila, and we headed to Wayne King's film premiere. The audience clapped at their own clapping, spanking their hands gleefully. Then to an after-party at a restaurant in the Strand. Donatella Versace hosted a party there when it first opened. My only memory of it is having a cigarette with her on the balcony and a wet rat scuttling over my bare toes. It had a slimy fur back and tiny pick fingers tucked up ready to jump. All while puffing on a curse-o-God fag, as Patrick Kavanagh's Mammie Flynn would call it. Tom looked up at the foamy sky and ashed in a Styrofoam cup. He ordered another round of tequila shots at the bar and brought back the spoils like Agamemnon returning with Cassandra from Troy. Loewe recently hosted a party here, too. The DJ spun the Macarena on vinyl and large plates of chips were passed around at midnight. It was like a children's party; the creative directors of fashion houses playing musical chairs. Below the restaurant, a twenty-something artist was staging his own retrospective. Sing a psalm and watch it burn.

The after-after-after-party took place at Tom's house, which still doesn't have any furniture. He was so spangled on starlight that even his sadness began drinking. Samira invited me on a press trip to Sharjah and then de-invited me, Tom invited me to a Wales Bonner sample sale but never followed up. Keshav whispered a secret to . . . Romy, put away your bloody Notes app. Decided not to drink anymore, handled everyone with the sensitivity of a professional art handler. Lay loin-facing downwards on the ground and listened to whatever anyone wanted to tell me.

8

We're halfway through the novel, keep going or go home early. Boredom of a relentless social life has risen. Gay men, amen. The sheer number of openings, dinners, and parties every night is excessive. It is as if the decision to host all these events was made at a time in the art world when everyone used to have fun. Now most people really look like they're here for work. For artists, especially the historied ones, these events are more of a chore than a celebration. They moan about having to attend their own dinner or party and make this known by spending most of their time at the bar or in the smoking area, white scarves of smoke blowing in the wind. Once, an artist popped out to have pizza next door during his own museum exhibition opening. The collectors are the people who seem to really enjoy these nights, because it's not work for them. Work is Deutsche Bank. Being Irish, having a good time doesn't require any philosophising. But for people in the art world, craic is less familiar. It's often a commitment. You know what else is a commitment? A novel. Reading often requires more commitment than any other art form, at least seven hours per book. But you're still here. You haven't been turned off yet. Read her fast. Read her slow. Read her again, intermittently. Pick her up and throw her back down. She loves that.

Paraded up Kingsland Road to DJ live on a radio station with a veteran sound artist. The radio booth is in Gillett Square, an area deeply rooted in Caribbean music, from block parties to venues like the Four Aces Club nearby, where acts like the Prodigy and Bob Marley performed. The alarms of all black people in Brit'n are timed to ring before the rest of the population, it is their destiny to be up at the crack o'dawn, wrote Sam Selvon. A prose technician who kept his contradictions close to his chest. My first radio appearance on Gillett Square was in my late teens. The set comprised two hours of Iraqi shoegaze and took place in the original booth, which has since been demolished. The local council are trying to push a narrative of regeneration over gentrification. Roses used to grow from the concrete but now all you see are glass shards. The Shard, glass drawing blood from those paid to build our modern colosseums. The artist had arrived early and knew what he was doing. This gave me the space to be hungover and ramble into the microphone. My idea of a perfect Sunday is watching a film at the Prince Charles Cinema, popping into the Jean Cocteau church next door, followed by dumplings at Royal China Club. Many friends tuned into the show, including Bushra, an up-and-coming starchitect, who invited me for a Sunday afternoon stroll in Hyde Park, a well-worn carpet underneath the sun. It is easy to forget that Hyde Park exists when you live in London. Many of us have escaped London for the weekend too many times on budget flights before realising that, actually, all we need sometimes is to touch some grass.

Hyde Park is pastoral in the sun, all dimpled cheeks and curls. The thought passed from my mind to murmuring lips. Bumped into a furniture designer wearing a Supriya Lele draped top and Birkenstocks, pushing an elaborate pram bearing a child with blonde pigtails. She pointed at the child. Not hers. The child scowled at me, and held a Black doll, which for some reason felt racist. Bushra was already sat outside Zaha Hadid's café, and we drank coffee in the shade. Shade is Dorothy Parker writing a book called *Men I'm Not Married To*, which listed the character defects of nine men she refused to marry. Or Sylvia Plath writing: don't expect any jealous letters pouring in to plague your bride, but let me nevertheless advise you—give her my novel to read in bed. Badass. And she read it, lying motionless between the sheets, like a health bar in a recyclable wrapper. Bushra was glowing and beautiful. Every time she opened her mouth to speak, the pigeons shut up so they could learn something. But Bushra is also troubled. (She has to be, because readers only like characters who look good on the outside if they feel shit on the inside.) We spoke about being surrounded by people but having unsatisfying social interactions, which is a lonelier experience than actually being alone. It is symptomatic of living in an big city, where disassociation is easy in a crowd, our feelings placed in storage. We are in a city full of women who have nothing in common with their bodies anymore. The alienation of city life has become even more pronounced thanks to algorithmic distractions. Scrolling away our emotions. The repetitiveness of turning pages. Social media has reconfigured our consciousness. It has become intrinsic to identity formation today. Fed by the feed. Be the most curious yet disaffected person in the room.

Even adult friendships can become a series of RSVP invites; relationships entertained at parties in the evening but never in daylight. Many romantic relationships are built upon convenience, and every winding street falls beneath the spell. Couples are often hard-launched at the outdoor pick-me tables of restaurants on Mount Street, where people go to pretend they don't want to be seen. Above Scott's used to live 'Groovy Bob' of Robert Fraser Gallery. Things were looser and more romantic in his day. The passionate tryst in Jean Eustache's 1973 film *The Mother and the Whore* today would be categorised as a polyamorous situationship. Many friendships in the creative industries involve something transactional, despite it being common knowledge that asking for something can create a power imbalance and impede the development of actual friendship. After all, everyone is in a room because of someone else. Caleb reminds me of this whenever he is angry with me. Sometimes he angers me. A few months ago a collector couple invited him to their *Architectural Digest* home. He demurred, telling me to go instead, because he was busy. You should have seen the panic on their faces.

No, no, you have to come too. They never even looked in my direction. But why the fuck would I have wanted to go? Maybe Caleb did it on purpose. Artists are often sincere and perverse at the same time. Picasso eats the apple, and the apple says thanks. Pick your battles. People who radiate the most tenderness and warmth are often those most sensitive to loneliness. The haemorrhaging of happiness: happiness is an amnesic because it helps you forget. My heart is rented on a long lease. It is full like the moon-shaped belly button of the sky, not yet on the wane.

We picked ourselves up and headed over to Alaïa, because when the going gets tough, the tough go shopping. People need to heal and also start dressing better. It's always when there is scant money in my bank account that the most pleasure is derived from spending it, either by splurging the entire amount on a pair of ballerina flats or buying random gifts for friends and family, like delicious big marshmallows from Fortnum & Mason. (Although you don't need money for a great gift: you need time.) Cue panicked scrambling to quickly earn it back, usually through freelance article-writing, although my outrageous spending habits are diminishing as my age goes up. Still younger than Jesus. Legs walked through the store and hands moved cash between purse and cashier. The medieval impulse to pay using cash. Pennies will probably soon be made extinct. If you're at a restaurant and it's cash only, you know the food is going to be good. Afghan Kitchen, Fryers Delight, Pelucci's etc. The manager asked if we were doing anything nice for the bank holiday, and we told her about our plan to go to the

Rio Cinema the next day. She asked if we were going to see the live-action *Little Mermaid* remake and we said no, *Sátántangó*. Swanning down Old Bond Street, we accumulated more shopping bags. A woman leaving a shop beside us crumpled her receipts into a ball and chucked them on the ground. Recognised her. We had sat next to each other at a museum dinner, surrounded by the Italian Mannerists and their smouldering Christs. She's a bloated Zionist who can't digest focaccia. Bushra told her to pick up her receipts, and she did. We assessed our early dinner options and ended up at a mahogany bar top on Brewer Street. Eating at tables is overrated, bar tops are more intimate. They make it easier to speak freely. Having a drink at the bar of a fancy hotel, a pair of elbows on the countertop, is one the most romantic scenarios. See the famous scene in *Waiting to Exhale* where Wesley Snipes and Angela Bassett share a moment, alone.

Bushra left me and my elbows at the countertop for a second dinner with another friend. She disappeared and skipped ahead a few pages, surprised to learn that my characters only feature as background figures in a landscape. You didn't even write about my outfit, she texted me. It was worn specially for the occasion. Next time. Promise? On God. Tom joined me and we headed for a drink at a pub around the corner and on a corner. My favourite publication is the pub. The pub is a solution to all of life's problems. Good day, pub. Bad day, pub. Why are all pubs in London on a corner? The Barley Mow, the Marksman, the Royal Oak, etc. The security guard asked for my ID on the door. Tom pointed at my shopping bag. Sir, these are Alaïa, no-one underage can afford these. A Texan couple sat at the table next to us asked us for a restaurant recommendation, and at the same time we both said Brasserie Zédel. It is the sort of place that our parents love. It felt good to just hang out with Tom at the pub. The best stage in a relationship is when you accept that neither of you will give the other more than what they are giving now. There were two underage kids snogging in a corner. What's your kink? Tom asked me. Dissecting privilege. The bad behaviour that can breed a Molly Keane. And you, what's your kink? Free market fundamentalism. Understanding how power is transferred away from public accountability and towards a free-wheeling transnational industry, outside the regulations or constraints of any single, governmental constituency. Skinny bitch? Yeah.

Travelled home and drunkenly reimagined the stations as Latin plant names listed poetically in the style of Derek Jarman's garden plants named in his journals. *Picadilius, Victorianium, Bakerloosa, Oldum Streetasa.* The new Elizabeth Line can get you from Shoreditch to Bond Street in ten minutes, the same length of time it takes to apply the LED face mask you've probably stopped using. The one that makes the girlies look like MF Doom. Tourists slow everyone down by rummaging for their tickets at the turnstile, standing on the left side of the escalator, entering the carriage before people leave. There was a tourist sat opposite me, wearing her backpack to the front. She squinted at the map of our city's subterranean world. She tried to wrap her head around the route and her lips around the syllables. The pool of her mouth occasionally opened to such generous proportions you could have swum in it. She showed us cavities of bougainvillea petals. People standing in the carriage pushed up against each other but experienced the bodily encounter indifferently. Capote's cold blood. There was a bleached head wearing a tie-dye Asai Takeaway dress. A modern London classic.

Many of the commuters did stuff like doomscrolling through the latest dooms, reading the same page of a book twice, and listening to music that bled through their headphones, drowning the screeching mechanicals. Close your book and open my wounds. The trembling hand of a man next to me brushed my right kneecap a second time. This was probably a very erotic moment for him. Checked the *Metro* horoscope. Speaking on the Tube is a form of verbal indigestion. It's uncomfortable. The only people trying to speak on the Tube are Spanish couples arguing loudly. The far side of them, two students with King's College tote bags. The girl was crying, a hydrangea of Kleenex under her nose. Her lips turned down like the dog-eared corner of a page. Just because you share a bed with two other people doesn't mean you're a communist, she said. There was a teen looksmaxer on my left, taking a selfie in the Tube window opposite. He clenched his jaw, his hand holding the phone so it would look strong and veiny. With him, a girl, who took a high-angle front-camera selfie in landscape with a 0.5 zoom lens. There was a man playing a tambourine. He was pretty good. The rest of us remain impassive, and we call it rest.

Indifference is a survival strategy, otherwise the sensorial stimulation of the rush-hour commute would be overwhelming. Disassociation is easy for my generation. Again and again, we allow anything to happen until we can't take it anymore. We know the moment to breathe and watch the world write itself. COVID-19 and Black Lives Matter and #FreePalestine before the age of twenty-one. Fetch the bolt cutters. The world has given us plot points with no story. Many spent their lockdown doing Chloe Ting ab workouts while a deadly virus seized the world. Online virtual viewing booths and NFTs had their fifteen minutes of fame. Twitch stayed. Too soon to reflect upon the emotional damage of it all, thank u next. We've gone from not owning our labour to not owning our minds, all of us lost somewhere in the uncanny valley of baddie content. Try living in the third person, watching your life instead of living it. Make important business decisions like you're doing it for someone else. Searched it. That's apparently called 'depersonalisation disorder'. It's more a basic condition of living in the city. Observing humans rather than feeling like a fully fledged human. Similarly, writing about the art world without writing about art. Avoid the interesting thing, choose the bullshit, and watch your brain rot. How do *you* bear witness to your life? Through Instagram stories? There's a version of my history where choosing happiness would mean choosing to write about art. When we retreat into a yapping of consciousness, where do we go? Stared at the blank pages of the afternoon.

My walk in the heat was sedate, and my thighs chafed beneath a dress which was flung off at home and replaced with a stained white vest and black thong. Flopped on the sofa like the *Decadent Young Woman After the Dance* painting by Ramon Casas. The woman has auburn hair piled in a bun and wears a long black dress. She lies down on her green sofa with an exasperated look and holds a yellow book, something like *Tales of the Ghetto* by Leopold von Sacher Masoch. She is unable to concentrate because she's too busy thinking about something or someone who causes her turmoil. Another diva on a divan. Picked up a book from the shelf and lazily scanned *Moral Tales*, a novel by Jules Laforgue, a Parisian bad-boy who influenced James Joyce and died young. The only way to read Jules Laforgue is to go straight from beginning to end. Alban Berg's *Lulu* was playing an aria for a sprigged hedge of bramble through my living-room speakers. Queued *Trapped in the Closet*. Organised a screening of it a few years ago in Beirut. Many Gen Z friends in Beirut told me that after the blast, they all became super horny. They started fucking like rabbits. The experience of reading a book alone on a warm night made me feel horny and restless. The same goes for a cold night. Spent the winter sucking icicles. Felt a dark and murmurous desire penetrate my being and fire me into brief iniquitous lust. Open app, scroll, double tap. Attend to the online commons (the comment section). Watch reel, tap for audio, laugh internally, send to Caleb, no new notifications, scroll more, refresh. No new notifications.

Threw Laforgue on the floor and picked up a book without words from the shelf. Played spot the difference with Hiroshi Sugimoto's sea of buddhas. Cigarette smoke dribbled through my fingers. Touched by the amorous sun, the stem of my spine arched from sofa to sea to see the sky, rimming the tide. Stars like toothpaste splatters on the bathroom mirror. The horniness became unbearable, my legs itched each other on the sofa, my nipples became hard and poked from underneath my sweaty vest top. When the nipple gets hard, the smooth skin surrounding it becomes wrinkled. It's a weirdly instantaneous ageing process that occurs and reverses itself within seconds. Pierced nipples look like butterflies on pins. Sweat purified by the divine blessing of an air purifier. A fan whirred anxiously. Stop virginating, Romy. Fingers reached between thighs which were plump and fleshy. Found my garden of Gethsemane. Caleb texted me about an intimate dinner, which meant fifty people in the upstairs of an art gallery. Stayed home, painted my toenails, and watched Pasolini's communist communion film, *The Gospel According to St Matthew*. Romy? A full-time *aonarán*. The radiator hissed a requiem and the crosses on the windowpanes prevented the devil from entering. Stars tugged through the darkness, pulled across the intergalactic shore from dusk to dawn.

This was all a poor attempt at a quiet night in, which for some reason proved difficult to execute. Just one night to reset, but that's exactly the night when the universe decides to throw a film premiere in your lap, and next thing you know you're sipping gin martinis off Curzon Street with Demi Moore and her chihuahua. Eventually, my restlessness longed for outside. My feet carried themselves to Teddy's house, a short walk away near Columbia Road. The air outside was dark and smelly as if the sky had worn the same pair of panties for a week. Gay winds caressed tormented young skin, innocent of tattoos. The walk to Teddy's house is a memory lane and a well-worn route which will take many years to forget. Teddy met me outside and leaned against the door frame, his hip jutting, a smirk on his face. His right hand fingered the lock and his left dangled a set of keys in the air. The first time the keys haven't been up his nose. His fiancé, Theo, watched him with a smile radiating complete reassurance in what made him happy. The key inserted in its hole scraped annularly thrice before the heavy fire door could be pushed open. Putting that into my corpuss. You terrify me, Romy, Teddy said drolly. You drink like a devil but you never miss a detail.

Teddy's friends were upstairs fanning themselves with press releases and yawning with the cathartic release of an *I love you*. One of them, who went to boarding school with Teddy, described himself as a 'creative director and multidisciplinary designer from Dubai'. The other was a chef at a fancy restaurant, where a two-backed beast was summoned in the bathroom two years ago by Caleb and myself during a gallery's Christmas party. She grew up in Harlesden, and her mum was one of the protagonists in *Babymother*, which is one of the most underrated London films. Theo was watching my favourite Christmas film in the background, *Eyes Wide Shut*. He wore a 2010s ready-made from Meadham Kirchhoff, or maybe it was Henry Holland. Boom clap. He who wishes for the cloths of heaven is currently working with a fashion photographer on his new project space in Camberwell, which Theo said would have a jacuzzi in the basement. Obsessed. There is an edgy new gallery nearby, which is more buzz than business. You should check out their current exhibition, Theo said. It's been extended. You mean nothing sold? We agreed that everyone wanted Christopher Kane to make a comeback.

The chef stood up, and her hand flew to her round stomach. You're pregnant again? Yes, must be something in the air. Yeah, your legs. Theo had stolen a BBQ which a neighbour had left outside on their lawn, and grilled chicken legs. He made all the meals and changed all the subjects. Teddy assembled lethal mojitos, pouring rum like water. Soon enough, he was racking up lines and asking me to twerk. He decided to make a plum pudding, which is often reserved for Christmas, but it was as good a time as any. He fastidiously followed the recipe. It flopped. The Worst British Bake-Off. Sentences are recipes for the reader. Let me cook. The 'creative director and multidisciplinary designer from Dubai' told us he is dating a guy with alopecia, and my mojito mouth asked if he was circumcised. *Dear Dick*, alopecia is not a religion. We stayed up laughing until one billion o'clock when our energy was reduced to embers like the BBQ's charcoal briquettes and the ashes of yesterday's eyeliner.

9

Last night my dreams combusted into the type of vision treasured by psychologists, an alternative version of history for victims of the waking world. The dream was set in my dad's birthplace during the war. My grandmother was in the dream, too. No-one will ever suffer as their grandmother suffered. She was in a ditch of dire poverty but wore her leopard print fur coat, the one she gave to me before she died. She lived the only dream she knew. Beneath the sun sweat soaked my skin and sand stuck to my legs. Slowly shaking the sleep from my body, my eyes opened on the morning. No-one is holy without suffering, a truth held close to my sore chest full of blood and guns. Dreams don't allow you to forget, you who dream and live inside the dream. There's a ghost of my life waiting patiently for me there.

Survived Teddy's mojitos and feigned control over the day by having breakfast, i.e. a double espresso. That was what could be afforded, at a marbled spot beside Green Park

Station. The one related to Café Baptiste. It was packed with politicians and wives, not theirs, their heads buried in the vaginal-pink spread of the *Financial Times*. Nobody for president. A shrivelled man slurped breakfast tea through thin lips which dribbled yolk and blotted the blushing pages of the newspaper. He had flaky-croissant skin. Not my cup of tea. A waitress brought a young man plain cereal. She poured milk, not hers. She looked like young Helen Mirren in *Herostratus*. Thought about telling her, but it was too early in the morning. Nannies beside the park entrance jostled with buggies in a mid-century jest. The *Financial Times* has pink paper because it was the cheapest option during the war. Mouth munched a flaky croissant and eyes digested headlines and infographics. Samira texted the YBF group chat: today is the fifth anniversary of Romy meeting Keshav for the first time in a dirty basement and telling him his belt gave Debenhams. Haven't worn it since, replied Keshav.

Samira informed us she will begin taking Ozempic, the slimming drug first popularised by celebrities attending the Ket Gala. My theme of choice for the Ket Gala would be no stylists. Just to see what would happen. Who are the people behind their stylists? Celebrities have become walking billboard advertisements for whatever brand they are strategically endorsing. The hot thing right now is to have a stylist more famous than yourself. Recently, a friend, embroiled in a scandal, could only afford either a great stylist or a great crisis-management team. She sloppily managed the full sordid details of her extremely public affair, dressed impeccably in Connor Ives. Keshav told Samira that she was just too lazy to go to the gym, unlike him. Shut up, Keshav. Samira, you look like one of those ancient goddess fertility figurines. You need to decolonise your mind. Khalas, Romy. Incheb. Don't tell me what to . . . Oscar was still tripped out in a ditch in the cruising area of Hampstead Heath wearing nothing but a Chopova Lowena skirt. The party was an annus anniversary of anus commemoration for George Michael. It had begun three days ago. He sent us a photo of men swimming like sperm across the pond. He had a threesome with two models, one was laconic and the other was catatonic. The streak of greasy sky visible through the window was already fried like bacon by the rising sun.

The arm of the clock budged, and a tour of tourists wound around the door. The waiter came with my bill, which signalled my time to leave. The sun boiled in the eggshell-blue sky. It was a good morning to sit in the Prince Charles Cinema. I saw *Goodbye, Dragon Inn.* My focus jump-cut between the screen and a bald head in front of me. From screen to bald head, bald head to screen. One of my uncles is bald. We used to crack open Terry's Chocolate Oranges on his head. Stepped outside to sun-rays, those umbilical cords of the sun. Trundled to a nearby members' club to answer some emails. Teddy and Theo were there, bobbing like rubber ducks in the pool. Hungover, we ate black miso cod for lunch. We played our usual game. Digestives or Hobnobs? Digestives, the chocolate ones. Stacey Solomon or Gok Wan? Gok Wan. Theo told us to stop. We were worsening his hangover. He felt like the lint at the bottom of a handbag. Keshav was tweaking out in his office nearby about a deadline. He asked if he could join, but we wouldn't allow him to. You don't need an iced blueberry matcha, you need to send the file.

Teddy was preparing his booth for Spoon, an edgy art fair in Los Angeles. It was for emerging galleries that hoped to graduate to the larger art fairs, once they're able to sell work at a higher price point. There are too many art fairs. Art fairs in Miami are like spring break for adults, where every party is a brand activation, an NFT launch or Narcan promo. Teddy only exhibits artworks that fit in his suitcase. Hundreds of scene kids ram the exhibition openings of emerging galleries, but these galleries often have only a tiny collector base. Most galleries are going to close in the next few years, Teddy said. How do you know? Tarot. The cards say it's dead out there. If his gallery fails, Teddy is going to go sell seashells by the seashore. Tom joined us for lunch. He had called into work lovesick. He brought a date for a vibe check. He was an emerged screenwriter in tiny swimming trunks, his pen on display. He told us he's working on an adaptation of *The Great Gatsby*. It would be somewhere between *The Great Gatsby* (1974) and *The Great Gatsby* (2018). We were all unimpressed. There's little difference these days between the dating and hiring process.

We rambled on about the scars of Giacometti sculptures and Richard Avedon's photographs of Andy Warhol's scars and the filigree of acne on my chin from having drunk all the mojitos the night before. Try Sophie's Choice BHA exfoliator, Theo recommended, presumably referring to the

Paula's Choice skincare brand, not the Meryl Streep film. The man at the table next to us had a rotund chow chow. Teddy petted him. What's his name? Mr Chow. The air-conditioning kept making me cough and sneeze. Teddy told me to stop acting like a diva. Air-conditioning always makes me ill. Illness means lying on the sofa in a stolen hotel robe drinking bone broth and ginger shots under the warm light of a lamp. Lips like a pillow and body like a blanket. The roots of my hair rhythmically pulsing with a headache to an inaudible bass. Illness means engaging in slow activities like reading Jon Fosse or listening to Galina Ustvolskaya or watching Lucille Hadžihailović films. Unlike *Scene City*, which is a reading experience more akin to scrolling, to passively consuming culture. This old building, my body. In London's art world people rarely know when you are ill. You just sort of van Gogh away for a while and then reappear and no-one ever notices you left unless you bring it up.

Headed to the noonday underground of legendary photographer Thomas Jameson's studio, where he was shooting a portfolio for a new fashion publication, founded by a well-known stylist. The photoshoot was as magical as all the famous footsteps that have walked through the studio door since 1985, when Jameson bought the building. Everyone calls him by his surname, including his son. Jameson sat in a wheelchair with a plaid blanket over his knees, a farmer's cap, and a failing memory. He still has a spectacular eye and a wicked sense of humour. He was assisted by his son and a young woman, but he himself still snapped the picture. When we first met, he called me Sophia. Sophia! He thinks you are his ex-wife Sophia Harcourt, his son whispered to me. It served us well, because a famous footballer bore the brunt of a bad mood earlier in the morning. The stylist lubricated me into a latex Alaïa dress, and Jameson asked why they dressed me in Durex. Are you fucking her? he asked Caleb, who wore an oversized Bottega Veneta coat, which Jameson loved. He looked at us both together for a moment. Apparently we were difficult together as an image. Someone apply orange lipstick on Sophia, Jameson said. Everyone silently exchanged looks as the orange lipstick was extracted from a coffee-coloured coffer and applied to my face. My face was met with a scrotumtightening sea of smiling faces when the make-up artist leaned back. It looked surprisingly good, but of course Jameson already knew that.

Jameson shared stories of wax and rosewood while trying to figure out the best way to photograph us. He mentioned the time he went to the British Museum with a sheikh. The sheikh convinced a senior curator to go into the vaults and find an extinct reptile to show his cobbler. Jameson also spoke about the time he photographed two legendary East End gangsters who ruled the backstreets in the swinging sixties. The charm of London is that all streets become backstreets after dark. It was only revealed to Jameson after the shoot that they were the same people who'd slashed his father's face a week prior. Jameson's father ran a popular nightclub in Hackney, and the gangsters saw him as their major competitor. There was a good film about the brothers, partly filmed in Café de Paris. We discussed the old British gangster film *The Long Good Friday*, about a Cockney crime boss who wants to redevelop the docks. Young Helen Mirren could get it. Didn't David Litvinoff work on it? Oh, my favourite East End film . . . *Nightbirds*. Jameson said that life in London used to be like that, conjuring all those ghosts of Shadwell Stair. Romy is a criminal, Caleb said. Why? She got fined £1,000 for watching Adam Curtis documentaries on BBC iPlayer without a TV licence. Okay, I'm reloaded. Jameson said that the street where we live is the same site where the first modern theatre was built in the late 1500s. Shakespeare, young and penniless, moved to Shoreditch. There's now a bronze statue in his memory near my apartment, which Essex girls on the lash can be seen humping at times. This famed theatre street now has a ball pit which doubles as a cocktail bar, but Jameson didn't understand what that meant.

Jameson motioned for me to sit on a stool with Caleb stood behind me, his arms wrapped around my arms. The heart is a light-sensitive medium, sliving and thriving and conniving. Someone tried to style Caleb's hair. When we went to see *Slave Play* a few weeks ago, an elderly theatre gay in the row behind us complained that Caleb's hair blocked his view. After the shoot, someone showed me a portrait of Jameson and Sophia from 1984. It was the same pose. In her hand she held his hand again. Her face was eyeless and shot with pink tinges of cheeks. Our pose made me feel secretly pleased. It was far more modern than the anticipated Elvis-and-Priscilla-type shot. The one where Priscilla kneels demurely beside or behind her larger-than-life husband. It is fine being in a relationship with an Elvis, two decades your senior, as long as he gives you the space to figure out who you want to be and doesn't have a problem with you growing into that person. Otherwise, the word divorcée has no business sounding so sexy. Me? An over-educated young woman who is best known in the art world for her boyfriend, partying, and tits. That's what it feels like, anyway. My mind pursues its phantoms. Squeezed into the art-historical role of Suzanne Mallouk. Women used to be anxious about how they look, but now we're more holistically anxious about how we're perceived.

The walls were lined with Jameson's photographs, including the one of Damien Hirst pulling his foreskin. There was a politician on the wall who Tom spotted having lunch last week with an OnlyFans model. It was at Sexy Fish or Bagatelle . . . Spare me the details, his wife had sighed. Did she have a BBL? No, but she looked like young Billie Piper. And she has a similar strategy to Israel. Which is? Continually pushing Western leaders' limits and discovering that they don't have any. Great, the wife murmured. She would write a novel about a crime of passion. Murder, deep throat. Conquer the diseased canker of his conker heart, we concurred. Does anyone have water? Sure. The hair stylist handed me a Diet Coke. In the time it took you to read this paragraph, Jameson's shoot was shot. We asked him which photograph was his favourite. He said he hadn't taken it yet.

Squeezed my body out of the dress like toothpaste from a tube and jumped into a cab bound for London City Airport. Again. Everything feels a bit surreal. It is difficult to have perspective on your own life. Sometimes our experiences only seem actual when they're projected onto a screen. Either way, we live our lives as if they were real. Never take anything for granted.

It was a quick flight to Antwerp, the home of artist Ida Ackermann, who wanted to paint me nude, swathed in clouds, for her upcoming exhibition. Ida sped us home from the airport with a cigarette between her lips. Her young daughter shot her arms skywards from the open car roof, screaming gleefully. Dark hair drooled down her arms, as she chevroned to her mum's mixtape blasting loudly. It reminded me of an image Tom made a few nights ago, when he rolled down the window of the car in a tunnel and smoked a Chinese cigarette. It was such a clichéd image that Teddy pulled him back inside with a look of disgust. Hey, don't include . . . Tom is far more cautious than the others about my literary endeavours. This annoys Teddy, because he thinks it compromises his chance at literary stardom. Tom is already going around town telling everyone he's starring in a novel. The YBFs have been reading extracts and suggesting certain details to add or remove. There will be nothing sensitive included. God Romy, stop being so lame. Teddy . . . It's important to keep checking in with everyone to make sure they all feel comfortable with it. By everyone, mainly Tom. The others are less sensitive to fiction. If they don't love the final draft, it will be rewritten. Friendship will always take priority over literature. Ugh, boring, Teddy eyerolled.

Ida lives outside the city in a farmhouse with feathered dinosaurs, mandarin ducks, duckweed, and short lotus stems. Sweeter than the country apple which greens upon the topmost branch. Atop the topmost twig a Thyrsis rests his eyes on the grass. She's the shepherd painter of pastoral elegies. Me and Ida first met through a mutual friend, the creative director of Alaïa, when he staged the runway show in his home in Antwerp. Antwerp and Ghent: what wonderful names, hard as the heavy cobbles in the square, says a man in Elizabeth Hardwick's *Sleepless Nights.* London is the city that sleeps. It felt unspeakably good to be in the countryside and away from the city forest of tall glass pines. In a cosy kitchen a home-cooked meal was waiting for me, which almost made me cry. Kiss the salty aphrodisiac falling from delicate eyelashes. The smell of tamarinds floated. Outside a grinning rabbit triumphantly held up every carrot he pulled from the soil. If trees are brown, then why is paper white?

We spent the night in her studio. Ida photographed my naked body posed atop a wooden stool. Thine eyes and on thy forehead gaze, suffering to be desired and blushed so to be admired. Putting the cunt in country, it seems. And some sort of muse, perhaps. The good thing about being a female artist is that you don't need a muse to get shit done. Being a muse in the art world today isn't about appearing in a painting, it's about embodying something that inspires the artist. Something that makes them want to be around you. That's my understanding of it, anyway. Amuse a muse. Muse is tucked into the word museum. O for a muse of fire that would ascend, the brightest heaven of invention. She was stacked. Oh, rack of enchantments! Many muses nowadays are self-proclaimed, with dragnet influence on a certain demographic, profiting from profanity. Gods make their own importance, and so does Julia Fox. It doesn't matter how you worship as long as you're on your knees.

Huntress of the depths of her eyes, Ida painted. An angel with winged eyeliner. Strange Halloween music from Eastern Europe played, heels clicked in a mazurka joined by the chirp of crickets outside navigating the darkness. Minor chords throbbed in the air. Ida carefully chose the wine in which we would drown. Her assistant flicked through worn books of Dürer paintings, and we looked at poses for reference. Occasionally we took comma breaks, during which we stayed hydrated with wine. My body warmed up with the assistance of a silk kimono and their family poodle sat elegantly on my lap. The comma, a halal moon on a blank sky. A tablecloth of smog masked the starry night, we smoked the polluted darkness, lit litany. Changed into a lacy Freudian slip at dawn, and fell asleep in a cold bed.

10

Flew back to London at noon the next day to deliver a guest lecture to art history students at Oxford University. Had to cancel an invitation to a lunch hosted by a popstar for his new nail-polish brand, a juxtaposition of commitments that didn't fail to amuse me. The evening plan, because there's always an evening plan, was a museum opening. My outfit was a denim leotard with knee-high leather boots. All Alaïa. Putting the cunt in *Künstlerroman*. Fits are important for fitting into my new life. The exhibition displayed bohemian ephemera belonging to the curator's famous nan. Her nan led an enviably hippy life, a revolution of evolution, which seems impossible now unless you're living in your family's real estate portfolio. Upon arrival, Samira's daytime trainers were quickly exchanged in a bathroom cubicle for her evening heels, a weary repetition of womankind. She threw her clothes over the cubicle door. Skims is Spanx for Gen Z. There was a gallerina doing lines with her friend in front of the mirror. Recognised her posh rasp. She works in a gallery just off Edgware Road. There's nowhere to eat near the gallery, she moaned.

Exiting the bathroom, Samira entered a conversation with a respected elderly critic who intricately knotted a neckerchief. What is your favourite cinema? He asked her. YouTube. No cap. He asked me the same question. Any of them. The best part of any cinema is that, unlike a laptop or phone, the screen is bigger than you. Size matters. The critic is a notorious cuckold, the bird that pops out of the cuckoo clock. He recently had a threesome with a well-known feminist critic, well-thumbed, who has *working class* in her bio. The only formerly working-class people who constantly feel the need to tell everyone they're working class are middle-class women whiter than their National Trust memberships. Both critics are swingers, an unfamiliar term to my Gen Z ears. It sounds like something vaguely dirty that people may have done in the 1960s. The impish T. S. Eliot line: who is the third who walks always beside you? He didn't pick up on my quote. The sweet cheat gone. Spied him later smelling his fingers as he furtively ran out of the disabled bathroom. Samira closely followed.

Everyone seems to have lost respect for critics. In his diary, published as *Of Walking in Ice*, Werner Herzog documented an insane journey he made on foot in the winter from Munich to Paris in dedication to Lotte Eisner, a film critic who was critically ill. Herzog was convinced that Eisner would survive if he walked the complete distance. She lasted another decade. The organs of snowmen have melted in city streets staining the shoes of suffering critics. Hosting is the new journalism. The violence of a content creator with a little microphone. Here's a novelist still working for your smile.

The exhibition had a diverse crowd, since non-profit spaces and public museums are more accessible than commercial galleries. Teddy was already there, with another friend from boarding school, Alia. How did you and Teddy become friends? Alia asked us. Teddy told Romy she was skinny, Tom interjected, who had walked over to join us with three beers. His mouth with sound had charmed my ear. Alia told me her father was launching his book on Edward VI, which he has been working on for forty years, at Westminster Abbey. This sounded extremely impressive, or at least far more so than my four-day plan to draft *Scene City*. Alia was the personality hire in an investment firm, working amongst men with lives scheduled and structured like TV episodes or stations of the cross. Romy has never had a serious job, said Teddy. No office skills, but she can scan a room. Alia's father's Edward VI project was an epic endeavour and quite important enough to have two nouns in the title, like *War and Peace*. There is a fine line between novelty and novelist, and it is in my interest to cross it.

Outside in the smoking area my hand tried to catch the raindrops before they landed. A cinematic gesture copied from *Hand Catching Lead* by Richard Serra. Does anyone remember when Oscar ate a cigarette for Truth or Dare? Keshav nodded. Keshav sucked his skinny cigarette so deep that it ashed to the filter. Where did you learn to do that? FIAC Paris, he replied. RIP, exhale. Alia had flexed her Westminster Abbey clout, but ultimately couldn't get married there because she's lesbic. Her girlfriend told us she was too exhausted to stay because her father had just been nominated for an Academy Award and—Is your girlfriend single?

Why does the art world get all the movements? That was the question being discussed upon my return inside. What do you mean? Alia asked. Zombie Formalism, for example, Teddy said. That was the 2010s. But the last major literary movement . . . Postmodernism. It began in 1945? Rubbish, Tom replied. There are tons of twenty-first-century literary movements, you just know fuck all about the book world. He's not wrong. Ask Romy, she knows her shit, Tom said. Please, all Romy reads is like, Laurence Sterne. He's weird and boring? Pouted and twirled the olive in my martini in reply. The essence of protagonists has changed. We are no longer action heroes but heroes of reaction. What's *Scene City* even about? Teddy asked. That's the reader's job. What's the reader's job? To generate meaning. That sounds lazy. No, it's true, look it up; Percival Everett or someone said it. Yeah, right. Tom joined in. She sent me an extract from her Notes app, she just goes on and on with her usual nonsense. It's called Dantean plurilinguismo, Tom. Is the scene city London? No, scene city is a culture state. Paused for dramatic effect and began: there's definitely been tons of local literary scenes. The B. S. Johnson era. He would have loved me. But they're not *movements*. And they were forever ago. There was Stewart Home, he tried to make Abstract

Literature happen. But it didn't happen. Alia looked at me. What's the difference between a movement and a scene? she asked. None of us said anything all at once. Movements have names? Was saved by a phone call from Ammé, a close childhood friend, who is not in the art world. Excused myself from the conversation and answered the phone. Hey Ammé, what's up? Hey Romy. Just read the midlogue and Notes app extract you sent me. (The Notes app extract: what would become Chapter One.) We have been close friends for almost fifteen years. That means my advice to you naturally carries more weight. It is this [redacted]

My phone died as Ammé began her book report. Charged my phone at the bar. In the meantime, miscellaneous friends invited me to various birthday picnics in Hampstead Heath. Forever 21, because none of them will grow up. There are no art-world parties in the summer, but everyone attends weddings in Patmos, Pantelleria, and Positano. Rich people holiday at the same locations and stay at the same hotels during the same seasons, as if they're on a school trip. In the art world, people get married a few times. Divorced beheaded died divorced beheaded survived. Socialites could wear trash bags at these weddings and *Tatler* would call them trashy chic. More runway brides running away from men; from Menelaus to Tom Cruise. At the bar an English literature undergrad was whitesplaining bell hooks. Woke boys lowercase and edgelords CAPITALISE. His parents were linguistics professors from Surrey, let's call them parentheses. Wokeness was colonised and transformed into a gross thing. Enough, Gagatha Christie, Keshav said, interrupting my thoughts. Someone had brought their dog, and Keshav petted it. Misgendering it led to some growling. (From the dog, not Keshav.) Kept yawning. Keshav told me to take a holiday. That would solve everything. But it wouldn't solve everything. The problem is me, a person who unfortunately would be on Filicudi too. My problem is a lack of discipline. Babe, you're locked in. No, the partying is distracting. Will the hedonistic lifestyles of my friends negatively impact their future? Not yet. Nervous breakdowns have been collectively postponed until at least a few of us can afford Ennet House or the Priory. Keshav told me to go on a city break. Oscar agreed, a weekend in Naples had changed him. What city changed your life? Wuhan. Spent most of the evening informing people about a film screening tomorrow. The Q&A would be hosted by myself and the lead actress, who had flown in from Los Angeles. Another Elgin House acquaintance.

The word *screening* is funny because it is bodily and cinematic. Mammogram, cervical, and film screening. Films are made for the screen, and we are living in a screen-dominated world. This should be a new era for cinema. The screen of my dreams is the wall that Richard Serra made for Joan Jonas in her loft, which she used to project videos during her 1971 performance *Choreomania*. The screening attracted a pick-and-mix audience. In the long queue to enter, a Central Saint Martins diaspora girlie spoke to a bald film archivist, who moved like he was P. K. Nair. He wanted bumpy cuddles, so he listened to her yap about Sofia Coppola's '90s TV show *Hi Octane*. Isn't that the same film bro who said you looked like Maya Deren? Samira whispered.

The actress arrived late with the daughter of a rock-star and ordered champagne from a delivery app which she drank onstage out of a ceramic teacup. None of these bitches are ever going to throw the first brick but at least they know how to throw a look. Samira fixated on the shoulders of the lead actress. She fingered a string of prayer beads with unreasonable horniness. Everyone nodded that the film was remarkable for its time. It critically addressed gender dynamics within Turkish middle-class society. Turkey used to be the centre of an empire, now it is the global centre for hair transplants. We celebrated afterwards in the pub. The actress failed to convince me to go with her to the Machine Gun Kelly party, which would have required fourteen lobotomies. There was also a prior commitment, a dinner at Frescobaldi's following an exhibition opening in Mayfair. Frescobaldi's is known for the pasta, but we ate chicken because the artist wanted chicken.

Spent the dinner chatting with a nine-year-old called Stella. She is the daughter of a Polish collector, who sat opposite me, named Malina. The only photo on my camera roll from that night is a blurry picture of Malina in her vintage Rolls Royce, with her driver, after a quick trip to small Tesco, just around the corner, to buy more packs of cigarettes. Children are far more relatable than adults. Not many people in the glamorous world of art and fashion and celebrity are relatable. It's funny when celebrities try and produce relatable content for their fans. There's a famous popstar, who shares a friend with Tom, who will enjoy a meal somewhere like McDonald's every two years or so. Each time, her order consists solely of a small portion of fries. She ensures the excursion is well documented by the flash of a pocket digital camera. The event always occurs after an award ceremony, so she's wearing custom Margiela or something. Her team will post the photos midway through the award ceremony carousel. This signals how, despite being a popstar, she is still relatable. She claims the act is authentic because she literally eats the fries. The same popstar has a sister who was recently released from prison. A news crew filmed her staggering out in frayed denim mini-shorts, a Jack Wills vest, Hunter wellies and a Barbour jacket, with blonde dip-dyed hair and a bindi on her forehead. Poor girl, Tom said when he saw it, she was still dressed for Glastonbury.

During the antipasti at Frescobaldi's, Stella scolded me for picking up olives using my long acrylic nails instead of a toothpick. She also scolded a curator for not washing her dog regularly and letting it run dirty around Aspen. Stella told me about the Harry Potter book series, which she is currently devouring, like so many before her. Too bad J. K. Rowling is a litigious TERF. Told Stella that Theo is the brother of the actress who played one of the lead roles in the film franchise. That means she kissed Harry! Stella exclaimed. The acting head of the acting department at Stella's lycée said she is going to be famous. The only thing stopping her is that she hates the idea of kissing anyone. Even someone handsome, she said. She scientifically calculated that by the time she became a rich and famous actress, she would have had to kiss three hundred men, and apparently that's not a good thing at all. Told her about my film debut, playing dead in a Yorgos Lanthimos film. Stella said that doesn't count, and there was me thinking it was iconic. Why aren't we famous? Stella asked. We're too morally ambiguous for the current zeitgeist. I'm nine, she replied. Stella snapped at a waiter because she was hangry. So was Bobby Sands, Stella, but he wasn't rude about it. Stella loves Caesar salad and absolutely hates pizza. What do you love? Matching sets. She asked about my credit score. Do you have a vegan dessert that isn't sorbet? The waiter shook his head.

Stella told me about her frenemy, which must be the new Gen Alpha term for school bully. She showed me a photo of the bully, her hair in an elaborate *intrecciato* plait. Stella never gets into serious trouble at school, because they have a four-strikes-before-detention rule. If you get the sillies, you need to go on a silly walk with the teacher up and down the hallway. The kids can do anything at all on these walks, even scream, so long as they get the sillies out. Stella only has one strike, because her teacher said look at me in one, two, three, and Stella did not look at her, but continued looking down at her Harry Potter book. Apparently magazines like *Girl Talk*, *Top of the Pops*, *Sugar*, and *Teen Vogue* don't exist anymore. Stella was sent home for wearing sunglasses in history class. She plays the recorder and does ballet, like most of us did as children but so few keep up as adults. Where did all our ballet lessons go? The girls still love ballet flats, especially from Le Monde Béryl. Stella is excited for the *Barbie* film, although she thinks the tagline *he's just Ken* is weird because that's not gender equality. If anything, she added, men go out to work, and women just stay at home doing nothing. Stella, that's not true! But it's true for my friends' mothers, she replied. She described a typical Holland Park wifestyle, with four kids apiece. Raising children is a lot of work, Stella, not doing nothing at all. Told her about the other Barbie, Klaus Barbie. Marcel Ophuls made a documentary about him, but it's quite different to the Greta Gerwig film, I added. Stella said she would watch it anyway. Stella watches children's TV in Warsaw on a monitor into which she can crawl. In the UK she streams content on Disney+. Told Stella that streaming hadn't always existed. If you weren't home, you missed it. For example, one time, *High School Musical* aired on the same evening as my school disco. Stella took one look at me. You went to the disco instead, didn't you? Children don't draw hopscotch with chalk on tarmac anymore and red telephone boxes don't work. Do you still do jigsaw puzzles?

The conversation was interrupted by a call from Ammé. Shit, forgot to call her back. Excused myself and went outside to talk. Sorry Ammé, got caught up. No problem, she said. Briefly, here is the advice promised to you on page 145. Feel free to write it in your own words. Now listen to me, Romy. Or if you're reading this novel, read me. There's so much going on for you right now. Too much to write. That's a problem, Romy. Because writing is what you can do. But no-one else is going to know that unless you do it. Start thinking of yourself as a novelist. Figure out what that means. Make your evenings less interesting. Begin ignoring invitations in your inbox. Do whatever it takes to make writing the most interesting part of your day. Forget the night. Or write about the night. Think beyond your PhD . . . How you even have time for that is beyond me . . . You need to start being honest with yourself. You're barely twenty-three years old, you do a full-time PhD, among other things. And you party every single night. The partying alone, from reading this novel so far, seems like a full-time job. This is my message: you need to begin protecting your ability to write. Because soon, you're going to burn out.

You offer readers a lot by giving them your view of the world. Even if there's no story, there's tenderness and humour in your voice. Even with your usual smart little tricks to divert attention away from yourself . . . Don't write a generic literary version of yourself that is vague and relatable enough to get you shortlisted for a Hooker Prize. Think about form. Develop a language to reckon with your existence. Stop trying to slip seamlessly into a scene just because you're a woman who feels like she needs to write herself down. You're only likeable because you don't give anyone much. Ouch. Wait. In the novel or outside of it? Outside of it. Your voice is not a character, Romy. It's more than that. But Ammé . . . Don't. Listen to me. Give yourself more of yourself. Give yourself more writing time. Figure out how to do that. So far, you're giving us a lot of insight into the art world, but not how you're coming to terms with the world as someone from the margins. Because frankly, you're avoiding yourself. Damn. Do you even want to be relatable to all the posh, generic, white women who are going to be reading this? Seriously, do you? Start writing for the people you want to relate to. You're writing in the wrong language. Pause. Ammé's breath huffed on the line. Will deal with myself more authentically in the next novel, when there are fewer hangovers. But there won't be fewer hangovers if you don't get your priorities straight! Hung up.

Headed inside and stayed sober throughout dinner. The madding crowd drank wine by the crateload until tongues loosened and nodding heads rested chins on clavicles. There was something quite punk about sipping tea from a china teacup in a room full of hungry looks. Did any figures from my peripheral vision suspect they were part of a novel? No, which made everything weirder for the characters who did. Abstaining from alcohol actually made the dinner more enjoyable. The experience of being hungover feels very 2010s. This decade is characterised by wellness and sobriety. There are a few millennial artists whose resurgence can be partly explained by their neater packaging of 2010s messy party-girl-with-cig hangover. They trade in aestheticised nostalgia. Gen Z can feel like they're participating just by listening to the music, without doing any of it for real. Stella, don't allow me to drink tonight, OK? You have permission to pinch me, like, really hard. OK! Becoming increasingly comfortable in these spaces has made it easier to not drink myself into obliteration. My role in these situations is usually that of listener, given my general lack of interest in discussing my own business. Constantly trying to control the raging intensity of my yap yap yap.

Sex and trauma are indispensable topics of drunken conversation, and people in the art world are no exception. There are very few people who get cabbaged at dinner and talk about art, unless they have something salacious to say about the artist. Discretion in the art world is highly prized, but as a result the gossip in art columns is excruciatingly bland. Scammers, forgeries, and divestments are merely a placebo for actual gossip, which, when the real stuff is available, spreads faster than a PDF before an art fair. Rebel without a pause. It's different if, like me, you were born into a generation that never had any privacy. Or if you grew up in an Arab houschold. You can't mourn what you never knew. Some gossip becomes news. There was discussion of a crotch-watching dealer and his infamous tea-bag trick.

Stella went to bed and a few of us went to Claridge's bar. Look at the night sky and clap for the stars. Seeking Soho, we then wandered towards its inflamed brightness, raw and itchy with neon signs. Towards the pub that only serves half pints, where Brendan Behan wrote *The Quare Fellow*. We ended up at the Harpo Club, which was so dull at this hour it felt like an airport lounge. Unlike Elgin House, the only thing people get horny for at the Harpo is a bump in the bathroom. Business here peaks at 7 p.m. on a Thursday night, when scoring a table or a bag on any floor becomes impossible. There is a renovation currently underway. Baumer & Baumann will probably try and change the artworks, even though the Harpo have their own large collection, traded with artists for a lifetime membership.

There are fewer permanent party venues than there used to be, and even long-standing parties routinely change their location. East London's queer art scene congregates nightly. The scene moves up and down Dalston like a hand job, constantly reinventing itself with every new lease termination. It produces a dedicated crowd of people who remain wedded to the scene for their whole lives, giving the parties a noticeably intergenerational mix. There are icons who've been on the scene since the New Romantics and still party for a living. A beloved drag and performance venue in Hoxton has just re-located further up the Kingsland Road, to a nightclub formerly known as Birthdays. Tom used to work behind the bar while interning for free at an East End gallery, which didn't last long. We were both London kids who became foreigners as soon as we entered another class, another version of our own city. We came up in Dalston at the same time. Except my time was mostly spent writing essays during the day at Café Oto. Tom said there's a new lesbian bar opening in Dalston with a Spanish name that means female truck driver. Raw fingers stroke carpels, quivering. Me and Tom often end up at a Dalston party after art dinners to shake off the social tranquillisers.

Headed to the venue. A drag queen was on stage belabouring a bear on stage. Ulysses, drag name Odysseus. The music was cunt and canticles interwoven in a communicant's prayer. Tom got accosted by a circuit gay who told him he was a whore. He said it as an insult, so millennial. Don't top a twink, just stop and think. You say that to everyone, he said. Yes, but it's your turn to hear it. Tom had ghosted the guy. In Tom's defence, he'd mentioned that he didn't want more than one messy night. The phrase *don't judge a book by its cover* is stupid because people show us exactly who they are. Sigh. Today we judge people by their worst behaviour. Their propriety takes precedence over their work. But it's more difficult to cancel someone who repeatedly and publicly states their opinions. Tom didn't build his success on an identity underpinned by the hypocrisy of liberal morals. We can blame algorithms for inculcating cancel culture in a generation, because we grew up consuming only what Big Tech knows we want to see. Meta is acquiring other companies. Metastasis. Social media has bred a lack of compassion for opinions and interests outside of our own. Meanwhile, tech founders, who spent their teens woefully struggling for the attention of hot women now have all the hot women in the world fighting for attention on their apps. Gross.

Teddy sidled up to us and asked Keshav about his catch of the day, an Iranian, a former waiter at Colbeh, who writes press releases for a grassroots charity. Is that all he does? Teddy asked, sloshing his martini. Write press releases? Bitch, imagine being a war refugee. Teddy closed his eyes underneath their Jimmy Fairly sunglasses and imagined. Ugh, boring, he said. During moments of global crisis, it feels wrong and wildly out of touch to live the way we do, whether we post our lifestyles or not, even when engaging in political action, beyond the phone and page. But at least we will never deny our own privilege.

It was the usual sort of a party where everyone outside wanted to get in and everyone inside wanted to leave. Drank a Diet Coke and puked immediately. My vomit was carbonated. Tried to find napkins, emptied a few Chanel lipsticks and dozens of dried roses from my bag onto a sticky table. Just here's fine. Teddy passed me a shot, Tom grabbed it. She's on the cordials. Midnight came, Tom felt his gibbous rise. His eyes latched onto a teenage boy in his catchment area. He was stood outside, watching a fox trot across the road. London streets are gross. Once walked barefoot across the Marais from an opening on Rue du Plâtre to another on Place des Vosges. My heels held in my hands while my toes marvelled at, comparatively, the surprising cleanliness of Parisian pavements. Teddy accidentally smacked my head with an empty coupe brandished in the atmosphere. Can a bear make me a cosmo? A former Maryam Nassir Zadeh employee, who now runs a record reissuing label, obliged. He invited me to an activation in Bermondsey. What the hell is an activation? It's an experience. You mean . . . an event? No, it's more than that. King Arthur spirited away to Avalon Café.

Hungover the next day, Tom still cycled to the office for work, like some *Avatar: The Last Bender.* Tom and Teddy, fond of a few drinks, enter another dimension when they're drunk. It's uncanny to observe. They become unrecognisable versions of themselves, like they've been hypnotised. My hangovers fare far worse. Find me on the sofa the next morning morosely editing my thesis with *Good Morning Britain* in the background. Click-clack my long red acrylic nails on the keyboard, listening to the presenters discuss the breaking news like whether or not Peppa Pig is a bad influence on children. Good night, China Chalet, Santa's Party House, GHE20G0TH1K, corpses which have begun to grow flowers. Good night, ladies, good night, sweet ladies, good night, good night.

11

Samira texted that she was in tears. She had been fired from her job. Her boss had to make budget cuts, and they certainly weren't going to be from his salary. She legit thought about taking it to the press, where she would recount the medieval travails of a corporate workplace. She was fired during *a cost-of-living crisis*! We told her to cool it. Her desk colleague, a West London girl, disinvited Samira to her birthday party that night at the Harpo. The phrase *West London girl* when employed by Samira was derogatory. London's swarm of WASPs. White women were less annoying when they didn't have any rights, Samira said. Some of them are good craic, though. Like the girls working at Baumer. They can get messy on a night out. Omg, are you siding with them? Samira typed into the group chat. Most of them are stuck in their head girl development stage, Keshav quickly replied. Or they behave like giddy labradors. Anyway, we're sorry, Samira.

Samira seemed more caught up in being uninvited to the party than in being fired. This isn't the first time Samira was uninvited from something at the workplace, which she argues boils down to racism. Samira was the only *other* in her department. There was so little *other* in her company that even the Polish girls began to behave like ethnic minorities. Nearly everyone in the educated creative classes needs to see themselves as a victim nowadays. Gen Z don't really care so much. We care more about, like, the imminent arrival of WWIII and being drafted. Not cute. Many racisms play out in the art world. White people go on holiday to the Middle East and ask me to recommend the best local restaurants and coolest art spaces. But when it comes to Palestine: *it's complicated*. People in the art world would never consider themselves racist and most of them would never mean to be racist. But many nevertheless repeatedly demonstrate a violent indifference to, and little understanding of, what it actually means to be a person of colour. They rarely have to reckon with their own privilege. Do you reckon? Yes, because the art world is structured around wealth and whiteness. Most white women in the art world publicly identify as feminists, but there's a huge lack of class and racial diversity amongst the women they choose to spend time with. Atrocity is our content and memes are our solace.

Samira, get your shit together and come with us to the Dérosian party. Tom works at Dérosian, the biggest of all the blue-chip galleries, so he invited all the fun people. Some dancing and pills would do Samira good. She already had an anodyne attitude from all the tranquillisers. Come out tonight and then on the weekend take a cheap flight to Marseille. Treat yourself. A cigarette and a spritz in the sun. Samira completely broke down before we even got to the Tube. Tears streamed lyrical prose down her face, as they did for the protagonist of Elizabeth Smart's novel *By Grand Central Station I Sat Down and Wept*. By Liverpool Street Station Samira Sat Down and Wept. She bobbed like a boat in a sea born of her own tear ducts with her weeping-willow hair dipped in the dirty pavement puddles. People stepped around her, late for something. Samira slumped against the wall of a Chinese restaurant with a large fish tank in the window. Jellyfish glowed under the water like stars fallen from the sky.

Joined her on the curb and sat with my forearms hugging my shins, elbows pointing outwards and knees pointing upwards. A bepigeoned brick wall cut the sky. We were women beyond recognition. Samira didn't know why she cried as much as she did, but her tears seemed to know. Maybe she cried for justice. Everyone in the office had made her feel so invisible. She whispered a secret curse of the Erinyes upon her enemies. Time passed. Get it together, Samira. Fuck that girl. Tell her to get stuffed, respectfully. And the rest? They're just basic bitches from the suburbs. They relocate to Hackney, act a bit quirky, trauma-dump online, and repeat. They're doing their thing, and seriously, good for them. But Samira, they've got nothing to do with you. You're a badass Arab woman, who has everything else to do with the rest of the world. Don't fool yourself into believing white women are at the centre of any relevant cultural phenomenon today. *We* are, and don't you fucking forget it. Oh . . . Alright. Pause. How was that for dramatic action? she asked. Not great, to be honest. You provided only drama. There was no action driving the plot forward. What plot? The plot where we do stuff and narrativise our lives. OK.

Samira rose, my honeyed tongue having dripped words to her taste. She would come party. Being a plus-one is the new being someone's girlfriend. We jogged down three escalators to the hellish depths of the Elizabeth Line and heard the train screech to the platform. Grabbed our tits and ran. Breasts flailed from the gaps of our finger barricades like the mechanical moles in that children's game. Whack-A-Mole. Bounce, fat balls. We made the train as the doors closed and her sadness became laughter, smoothing roughness like Vaseline. Only an Irish sense of humour can make such a glad time of chaos. At Bond Street Station we dodged a twee feminist in a pastel suit with pick-me energy. She gives me a fucking headache, Samira muttered. We took a detour to Maison François for a consolatory glass of pastis, which reminds us of arak. Hoisted ourselves onto bar stools. Sometimes none of it feels real, Samira said. The pastis in front of me is real. Us going for a drink is real. But something about it feels . . . unreal.

This is a novel, Samira. It's not real. Although everything that happens in a novel should probably feel real for the characters. So, uh, my bad. That's not my point, Samira replied. My point is to draw attention to the unreal nature of the world we live in. Even if most of what happens is so normal for us, it's probably incomprehensible to most readers. Hell, many of the super-rich people we know, she said, have never even *spoken* to a normal person, beyond cursory exchanges with their personal trainers. The unbelievability of our lives is a constant suspension of belief. Samira is right. Having perspective is a way to stay grounded. Writing down problems also shifts them *over there.* Some of us have had to travel far in experience from our families. My problems in this new life are outrageously privileged and infinitely preferable to those faced by my family. So how do you write a novel without alienating your community, and remain true to your experiences? Samira asked me. Well, this novel unfortunately isn't set in that community. Meaning, the community of my childhood. So, who is *Scene City* for? It is for a niche of people in a flashy world formed by conditions outside of it. The narrator in *Slaughterhouse Five* said he was going to write his war book first and his fun book second. So it goes. This novelist is going to do it the other way around.

The group exhibition at Dérosian featured hit singles from each artist. There were many people in the gallery who seriously contemplated the paintings. Everyone gave the paintings what they needed, flowers bending to the sun. Where the most zealous congregation has people speaking in tongues, we speak in press releases. There were many socialites, including Marian Leatherby. If she were a canapé, she would be cold-creamed asparagus. A standout work was Bianca Jagger's gorgeously styled hair, which bounced vivaciously every time she walked. Hair volume is a measure of time in Sofia Coppola's films. Marie Antoinette's hair explodes as she gains power, and Priscilla's hair shrinks as she grows into adulthood. Bianca still wore a COVID-19 protective face shield. She is interested in the young arts scene. Last year we walked around an art fair together, and she wanted me to introduce her to some young artists. We both had uncomfortable shoes and stopped at each booth to sit down. A royal photographer once told me a story about the time he escorted Ms Jagger home because her shoes were uncomfortable. She is a profound woman with a light step whose public image as a style icon overshadows her decades-long activism in various war zones. She is best friends with the chicest gallerist on the planet, who surrounds himself with women who have no split ends and float two inches off the ground. He hosts dinners at Maxim's, an art-deco fairy fortress in Paris, and wears monogrammed shirts. He once took Basquiat to the opera in Austria, where Basquiat fell asleep. He adores glamorous women and once bought all the women in his office Louboutin stilettos for Christmas.

Back to Dérosian. In a congregation of navy suits, Arabella wore a pink bouclé jumper. It was the exact peculiar neon pastrami shade of a Philip Guston painting. This was culturally significant: the last time someone in the art world wore a memorable colour was Tom in pale-lilac raiment, a Marni shirt with detachable ruffle. The other image of lilac nested in my memory is the Groovy Chick beaded curtain which hung from the doorframe of my childhood bedroom. Or the lilac trousers worn by both Denis J. Maginni and Tom Kernan. Lilacs out of the dead land, the turn towards quiet luxury ushered forth a condom-coloured camouflage of Loro Piana and the Row. Conformity masquerading as luxury. Everyone wore the same ballet flats, the ones with diamanté studs, and a Le Teckel shoulder bag. My thoughts are always the same colour as my clothes, says Lilian in the André Gide novel *The Counterfeiters*. There is no-one more stereotypically French than André Gide, with his ruminations on middle-class moralities, which are similar to those prevailing today. Except, the form of cancel culture practised by the educated middle classes has become one of the most oppressive moral policing practices in the panopticon of liberal society. French reading list: the Alain Chartier to François Villon to Arthur Rimbaud to André Gide pipeline.

Dérosian had invited this person and that person and all the others that one sees all of the time. You rarely spy anyone new at the more glamorous openings, dinners, and parties, unless it is someone from out of town, such as a visiting gallerina who works with the same artist in another country. The artists will sometimes bring friends from fashion or music or film who would feel comfortable in the social context on offer. Most people attend to be seen by the same people who see them all the time. How are you? Grand thanks, you? Yes, very well. Did you catch the biennial? Yes, we're a decade away from a meme account curating the Whitney Biennial. Lol. And did you see—Yes, I hated it. Why? Oh . . .

The girls were alert: a stunning twink stood alone in front of a Jadé Fadojutimi painting. *Tutto sciolto.* He wants to fuck me, Keshav said. How do you know? He invited me on a studio visit. His name is Simon, like simony in the catechism, a simoniac of his sin. Simon was six feet five, and in terms of scansion, he was more than a hexameter. His eyes were brown or something. His bio? Digital nutritionist and artist. The type who posts semi-nude selfies in front of their artwork to boost engagement. Why didn't you hook up? His twink handler didn't approve. He looks like Lil Nas X, said Oscar. Just because he's Black doesn't mean he needs to look like someone, Samira said. It's always trashy twinks with manorexia who have the most debonair in a chokehold. But everyone can be hot these days. It should no longer be an asset. It's all going to be about body modification next.

There is lot of posting during openings. People on the periphery of the art world post everything that they go to see, as an indication of status, whereas people working in galleries only post what they think is good. Simon stood in front of the painting because it matched his outfit. He wore Charles Jeffrey's Loverboy, which is Vivienne Westwood for twinks. Who's *that*? asked Oscar's friend, Emerging Artist #1. Emerging Artist #1 was a Vaseline muse with an unexpected item in the bagging area. A Comme des Sapiens from Oklahomo with an accent resounding flatly like feet on tarmac. Oscar brought Emerging Artist #1 because he wanted to be in the novel. What did you just write? Some people have become wary whenever they see me open my Notes app at a party. Emerging Artist #1 beckoned Simon over and filed his own fingernails. Emerging Artist #1 and Oscar and Simon took to the bed. Steal a painting from the wall, make a kite of it and fly.

There was Emerging Artist #2 projectile-crying outside,

I should have been in that group show. Last month he exhibited a single painting, which he asked us all to photograph at his opening. At the end of the night he destroyed it, so the artwork became the camera roll images. Boring. Technically, he doesn't even qualify as an emerging artist. He's over twenty-seven. Being an emerging artist should have less to do with age, more to do with how long someone has worked as an artist. Regardless, he's lame. He used tears instead of saliva to moisten the glue on his rollie. Keshav stared at the chorizo stuffed in his skinny jeans. Emerging Artist #2 pretends he has a waitlist, but Keshav saw his unsold artwork on an online art brokerage. Keshav was being salty because someone at the office exposed him and told everyone that he, too, was over twenty-seven. He usually told people he was twenty (the seven was silent). Thus his subsequent becoming a twonk, a twink in the past tense. He skipped gayly on twinkling shanks to hail a taxicab to the after-party, molten pewter jewellery jingling.

A performance artist named Emerging Artist #3 joined us in the cab. She puts the star in starving artist and embodies the balletic poise and pose of a young Quentin Crisp. Emerging Artist #3 recently became successful, but no-one cared until she rebranded as struggling, then everyone wanted her. She was from the +212, an Upper West Side girlie whose art school tuition was paid by her parents. Oh, you're from New York? Name every rat. Tom asked what made her want to go to art school. Tom himself went to art school but retired his artist career after graduation. His graduation video was the Twin Towers exploding to a soundtrack of male pornography. My generational trauma of suburban angst, Emerging Artist #3 replied. Then she decided to become a sex worker, like so many edgy white Jewish girls before her, from *Working Girls* to *Slaves of New York* to *Shiva Baby* to *Anora*. Moon-dew stars her wet lashes, back and foot and brow arching. She did it to feel real, to be desired, to rebel against the system, to form an identity beyond her community, she said.

Why is a slice of pizza in New York more filling than a whole pizza in Europe? Do they really eat donuts over there for breakfast? Emerging Artist #3 brought along another artist, a laconic waif from Ludlow who is just coming to terms with it all. OK so, Bruce Nauman is the guy who did, like, the famous performance videos, or Vito Acconci or whatever, or was it what's-his-name Vito . . . Whose dad makes like, film films . . . They have his paintings in the Dior store . . . Chris Ofili this, Peter Doig that . . . And then who is that guy, who abbreviates his name to AJ . . . She thought Pipilotti Rist was a fashion brand, Emerging Artist #3 whispered. Iconic, tbf. Then Teddy told them his childhood story of how he was cured of cancer by seeing George Michael on TV.

The after-party was at a country-style mansion tucked into an enclave of Holland Park which Dérosian had hired for the night. The ceiling wore chandeliers like earrings and resembled jewels worn by guests, fragments of slipping reflections. The shadows played a crepuscular opera against the walls, between which buzzed a hive of London's glitterati. The women were as light and rich as their Augustinus

Bader moisturiser, eyes impersonal in the absence of desire. Barrier moisturiser is important in London, what with all the smog and cigarette smoke that gets blown in your face. Samira was a far cry from all the crying now. She was in a corner sucking the face of a Silicone Valley guy, machine yearning. Suck is a queer word, wrote Joyce in *Portrait of the Artist as a Young Man*. He compared it to the sound of dirty water going down the hole in a basin. Then he called the taps *cocks*. There were two cocks that you turned, and water came out, he wrote, which is presumably the Irish humour we talk so much about.

Meanwhile, Emerging Artist #3's friend (Emerging Artist #4?) was in the bathroom queue scrolling through Teddy's account and telling him that he wasn't c-boy enough for Dimes Square. She wore a nip-waisted baby tee from Com Tees and squinted at Teddy above tiny rectangular glasses. Who do you want to see when you're out there? Teddy said he had seen enough. Subject line, Teddy's upcoming trip to New York. Teddy said he doesn't give a fuck about those try-hard fags. Anyway, he would be at an art fair booth all week, you know, working. In Europe, the most affluent social media presence is a private account with only a few hundred followers. Quality, not quantity. Mysterious on main, active on Close Friends. Wink. Emerging Artist #4 looked at him baffled. Teddy stared him up and down, from head to legs, the split ends of the body. For who approves, the narrator quotes Petronius without attribution, of conduct unlike her own?

Classical sculptures guarded the roses in the garden. A

vaping Phidias gazed at cream curves of stone as if they were flesh. Through open windows the soft breeze stirred the shoulders of fur coats in the bathroom. The glamorous myth of the emptiness of such a night is the bait with which crowds are drawn. The canapés were so delicious that no-one knew what they were, and champagne flowed from every direction, poured into flutes on which mouths could make music. Samira rubbed champagne into her pores, sweaty from all our dancing. She was a hard shell of an oyster with something good inside. Someone's necklace snapped and spewed pearls over the dance floor. Expectation clogged the air like blackheads. The ballroom was packed tight with politely reciprocal curiosity and everyone spoke and said nothing at all. Nothingness is taking over the planet, which is something. My favourite small-talk topic is asking collectors which pieces they choose to display in their bedrooms. Someone with a prestigious collection told me they hung a Jordan Wolfson painting above their bed. (Said collection is in a storage unit in Geneva.) A successful artist told me he sleeps on a mattress he designed, with another version in a museum. A few years ago he cheated on his wife in a very public affair. His blatancy and lack of shame left people wondering whether it was part of his studio practice, especially since he exhibited blown-up photos of the other woman's naked body at an art fair in Seoul. It earned him blue-chip representation and a divorce. His wife bruised his chest with a chisel. He hadn't even brought her back any Korean face masks. Before that performance, he hadn't suffered enough to be an art star. Jesus loves a sinner, and so does Levi Dérosian. The artist is now having a midlife sexual crisis, pining after young art hoes in the manner of Lars von Trier, who posted an open call for a girlfriend/muse on his social media account. Hot is and hot does. Especially if you're full-frontal fine. Remember when being poly meant Polynesian?

There was virile excitement in silences tucked between couples huddled in the corners, trading his and hers for hymns and heresy. Sexual tension reverberated like an acoustic resonator amplifying a star. The fourth most interesting Rothschild had a large purple bruise around her eye which she alleged was caused by an Auguste Rodin death mask falling from the wall onto her face during sex. Her original form was unidentifiable beneath all the silicone. She was sloshed and had more on her mind than these pages allow, and then introduced me to her special friend, who was looking for his biological mother. This is Romy, she said, she is the GOAT of satire. Don't you mean S-A-T-Y-R? The special friend told me all about their upcoming biennial, which will be so bi. An auctioneer with a bulging crotch and a red phone case pressed to his ear shimmied past us. He was front-loading, for sure. Outside, the image of a truck and the voice of a woman went by.

A balloon floated up into the sky and became a moon, and we rushed to the end of the night. No time to drink tea or wait for it to cool. Just before dawn a few of us headed to Elgin House. The doorman at the back entrance saw us and let us in despite the queue, which was as long as any at an early-morning Next sale. Elgin House was full of content creators in wet-look dresses and injected lips, perched on the laps of uninterested men who all looked vaguely familiar. The scene evoked a tabloid headline: Famous Actor Hides Behind Face Mask to Join TWO Stunning Models. Dérosian once rented out the entire building for an artist who wasn't even there, or at least Caleb couldn't find him. Levi Dérosian was sat in the corner with a bunch of antique men and looked like a real mafioso. At the bar, a man in fintech told me he was in the process of convincing a porn site to invest in AI. This was to more seamlessly present preferred videos through a personalised algorithm. Right now it's like flicking through the bloody TV guide, he said. *I don't want to browse, I want to bust*. The most desperate people in the world can be found at Elgin House in the early hours of the morning.

12

The next morning Samira received a message on Microsoft Teams from a colleague saying that the party at the Harpo was empty and she could have got in. No worries, she replied, I went to the Dérosian party instead. It was fab! Go off. *OUT* West London girls, *IN* literally anyone else. Everyone in the YBF group was active, except Oscar, who was still asleep. He set two alarms in the morning, one for the person he was and the other for the person he wanted to become. Everyone is the same, wrote Teddy, some blow and a Brompton bike, waiting for life to happen. My shower became drenched with water and so did my body below. Meticulously washed the inside of my ears like Jeanne Dielman. Just shampooing my hair these days feels like a glow-up. Thought about the concept of name-dropping; a literary device, if Victor Shklovksy is to be believed, because it's alienating and depersonalising. To better understand what's in front of us, we commodify it. Similarly, dialogue can lose its narrator and camouflage into the environment. Speech can lose its marks. Dialogue is often used to mask feelings. We place too much emphasis on its importance. But this is a landscape study, baby. How we see things is very different to how we feel. Believe it or not, there's psychological depth to the characters in this novel. But if everything about them was exposed, there'd be no art to make, no secret desire. Life would be in an open relationship with the world. The art world is optical, and its speculation emotional. We're in a world where words breed more truth than images. Time we began judging people for how they narrativise themselves. Isn't that what you do on social media? You're the person you choose to show me. Pause. How can meaningful life be obliterated further? the showerhead asked. With a soundtrack, my wet head replied. *Scene City* and a G string.

Shower thought: recently watched Pedro Almodóvar's *Kika* with Caleb, which was great. It was camp and stylish, as if John Waters was in '90s Spain. But it would be impossible to make a film like *Kika* today because of the incest and the comedy rape scenes. There's a critical tendency to project today's morals onto historical figures, and we're doing the same with fictional films. A tragedy of contemporary culture is that it won't allow itself to be messy. Different cultures used to be for particular audiences. Every artwork shouldn't be for everyone. Know that something can hurt you and still have a right to exist. Culture becomes policed because certain people are triggered by an old film that has nothing to do with them, and so culture becomes the most watered-down version of what it ought to be. It's crazy that a literal film on a screen can be deplored as violent, when there's so much real violence in the world . . . That's why Hollywood is pushing soft boys of the Jacob Elordi ilk. Hyper-macho men trigger liberal Hollywood. It's class fear, and it reminds them of working-class people who potentially voted for Trump. Then there's the indiefication of Hollywood. Hollywood latched onto the indie aesthetic for integrity, just as it was introducing AI. Indie filmmaking is where genuine micro communities existed. But now 'indie films' can look like the thing without being the thing. Still they tell us to join them, and call it representation. Representation is dangerous in these systems because it enables appropriation. Caleb joined me in the shower. And don't get me started on the bullshit way representation has been linked to inclusivity. *One* Black woman will be cast, usually as a love interest to a white man, and she'll be the most beautiful and accomplished woman anyone has ever seen. And isn't excellence *exclusive*? Caleb nodded. Anyway, your generation's take on identity is cooked. Caleb said he wasn't a millennial. Apparently, he is Gen X. Whatever.

Up above? The sky was baggy. Stared vacantly at the boring ground. The River Thames needs a rebrand. It could be cool, because it's dirty and dull. But it's not. The dizzy evening repeated itself. A painting exhibition opened on Bury Street. The cab ride took forever, another traffic jam outside caused by another television production crew shooting another period drama. Thirty minutes later, the car belched into a parking spot. It was a sweaty evening, and bodies crowded into a small space which reeked of beer and boded terribly for hangovers among the attendees. It smelled like the scene in one of the paintings, a sexy take on *At the Moulin Rouge* by Toulouse-Lautrec. Disassociated at the opening by staring at the art. We disassociate to cope, because remaining in our bodies is to remain in agony. But some people lack the dissociative skills needed to emotionally survive the apocalypse, and it shows. There were great cats lurking in the corners of her paintings, cats arching their backs under the roof of an arcade. I have about a hundred cats living in me, and all of them are curious, wrote Kathy Acker. There was a heavy Bottega Veneta bag on my shoulder full of books on the Suez Canal. This is hardly a novel, it's an exercise in product placement, Ammé texted, and you're not even getting paid! An Italian socialite complained to me about her husband, whom she had met by looking lost at the Principe di Savoia. She suggested there should be a book about artists' wives, though it could never be more amusing than Françoise Gilot's book about her affair with Picasso. Dating a male artist is an Olympic event, long-distance with many hurdles.

Downstairs, in the gallery office, a visiting artist from Los Angeles was laid out on the viewing room sofa, too hungover to cope with the heat and the beer stench upstairs. He looked like a Christ in an El Greco painting, elongated on the sofa and pigmented by alcoholism, if Christ were gay and wore Carhartt. He's one of those small artists who make big paintings that take a long time. He gasped in the sort of gay way you only see in Hollywood films. Unruly hair, no make-up, Bella Freud 1970 jumper, oversized houndstooth coat,

Phoebe Philo loafers . . . You look so . . . *British*. Goddamn it, I'M IRISH. You are the Jeanne-Claude of male crushes, he told me. What does that even mean? My body flopped down beside his on the sofa. And who the fuck is Jeanne-Claude? Back upstairs, Tom, still on Dérosian hours, was pacing on the phone, wearing gorgeous vintage crocodile shoes. The only people with two phones are dealers, either drugs or art. Even if you're no-one in your own right, you can attain a powerful position by joining the corporate ranks of a mega gallery. Same goes with a cult or a terrorist group. Are you saying a gallery is a terrorist group? Tom asked me accusingly, pausing his call. Tom, there's no space in my low word count for your mock outrage.

The after-party occurred at the same Mayfair institution where Prince Andrew and Virginia Giuffre allegedly met. The venue was chosen last-minute because the Maison François toilets had flooded. Someone probably clogged the lavatory again. Everything happens in the downstairs bar of Maison François. Parties happen all the time and they're pretty much all the same, but many have witnessed collectors and patrons getting totally furious if they're not invited. It makes sense why they would feel upset. Part of the exchange of financial patronage is to access a certain lifestyle alongside creative people like artists. Successful artists often make themselves as inaccessible as possible. Back to tonight's members' club.

The interiors involved birdcages hanging from the ceiling, which contained fake fluffy bird, and made the establishment extraordinarily camp. The maximalist aesthetic of velvet sofas, patterned wallpaper, and dark lighting is characteristically Mayfair. All arses and arrases. Someone, obviously an artist, tried to steal a tacky Piero Fornasetti coaster for the hell of it, but she got caught, and then the waiters removed all the coasters. She wore a Nicholas Daley hat, and fine strands of curls fell down her cheeks like wet mascara. She was now a successful painter, following a short modelling career, and brief exposure to photography.

A painter sat in the corner was gutted because the waiter wouldn't bring him any asparagus, which kept being eaten before the silver tray could reach him. He suffered in the furtive intellectual way of Emil Cioran. Talk sailed into rarefied waters, on a snub-nosed boat, as we spoke of moon-sweet madrigals and oratorios and babies, which we don't want. A painter beside us had just returned from Simonetta's private island. Gossip spread through the room like a yawn, including the rumour of a love triangle between a woman artist who was there, a billionaire, and a former prime minister. The billionaire was once a mathematician, the sum of a sigma male. He said his favourite authors were Charles Bukowski, William Burroughs, and Jack Kerouac. He asked for my favourite authors. James Joyce, Julio Cortázar, B. S. Johnson, David Foster Wallace . . . No women? he asked. *Ain't I a woman?* Omg Romy, shut up, Tom muttered. Anyway. It would have been far more scandalous if the artist were fabulous and stopped shying away from the news as if it stained her feminist credibility. Too shy, too shy. Bring back the days when women paraded naked on horses to prove a point, like Lady Godiva, who became the muse of a chocolate brand. Oh, the genitals of gentiles. Yawned. Asked Tom for the time, my phone was charging at the bar. He looked at his wrist, realised he left his Apple Watch at the sauna, and so he just looked at his wrist. (Michel Houellebecq is the best author to read in the sauna.) As a child, Tom was almost cast in *Billy Elliot the Musical* but was rejected at the last moment because Elton John said he was too gangly. Instead, the role went to Tom Holland, meaning that if our Tom had been a foot shorter and heterosexual, he could have dated Zendaya.

It was permissible to smoke inside so everyone stole Tom's cigarettes. You're only a smoker if you buy your own. There were corpse-like qualities to the empty cigarette packets thrown on the glass tables. Crush empty packets of cigarettes in your fist like John Chamberlain. Due to my abstaining from drinking, the other option was drinking coffee, smoking, and having deep conversations. Espresso tonic washed around my laundry mouth like sodium carbonate, followed by a deep drag of my lipstick on a cigarette. Wait . . . Tom interjected, having a tipsy moment of clarity and being familiar with this paragraph, since it is about his cigarettes. You don't even smoke, Romy. Um, yeah? No, you don't. This is fiction, remember? Ugh, whatever. Holding a cigarette is a devastatingly romantic gesture. It always was and always will be. That's a fact of life. Joan Didion looked so narrative when she smoked. Those black-and-white photos of her smoking, staring straight into the camera, straight hair tucked into her jumper . . . Smoking in a novel isn't going to give me lung cancer. Not unless Romy decides Romy wants to die, Romy said about herself. Poor Romy, Tom replied, rolling his eyes.

Tom introduced me to his former housemate, a Renaissance-style model, who told me about her sci-fi novel idea set in a not-too-distant future. It follows the repercussions of the government's plan to make everyone asexual to increase productivity. She asked about this novel, my *sub rosa* story of visions and revisions, which Tom had told her about. Except he couldn't really say much, because there's no story. It's about an art history student who tries to find a purpose in life and ends up writing a book, he said eventually. Put that on Publishers Marketplace. Tried to think of my own answer, but the sentences became bruised words in my clotted throat. Gagged. Stuck-up, rub the starch out of me. Threaded some beads of words together to form a rosary, but it felt odd trying to speak about my ideas. Despite the sociality of this novel's content, the novel form is a silent phenomenon. It's also just plain difficult trying to speak about your own work. In fact, it's much more interesting to discuss the process rather than the meaning or point of it. How many copies do you hope to sell? she asked. As many as the number of words in the novel. Then each person could claim ownership over a word, a double-entry accounting recompense for reading. And what genre is it? she asked. The restless genre. That genre doesn't actually exist, she replied politely. Oh.

Freshness of words and simplicity of emotion. That's me. Writing words is easier than verbalising them, and so the novel form only enables my cowardice. It is relatively easy for novelists to be vulnerable, because in silence you can say anything you want. Those who really speak their truth out loud are rappers. They even call it punching rather than writing, without hiding behind words on paper. It is easier to write the words you dare not speak. Words are vehicles but they also pull the brakes on desire. The words chosen for my mouth are very different to the internal yapping of consciousness, this ceaseless language of thought which torments my brain, that which is being written and which you have taken to reading. Yet, these sentences are strangely starting to sound better than the ones that come out of my mouth, standing on unsaid business at the foot of a sentence on the edge of words.

Tom, meanwhile, was trolleyed and telling an audience of collectors about the time he stood in a six-hour queue in Chengdu for a selfie with a panda. What turns you on? someone asked. Institutional affiliation. Tired, the rest of the words lay asleep in my mouth, snoring beneath the rough blanket of my tongue. The tide of day was near its turn, time to retreat with a wane. Tired enough to dream of sleep in my sleep. Tired all the way to a vague closing time in a warm haze of cigarette smoke, listening to the comforting sound of chatter. My eyelids drooped in a performance of the setting sun. We all went home, and some people's daughters drunkenly detoured down Piccadilly into the Tiger Tiger nightclub, burning bright in the forests of the night. The sharp shingle of an organic wine bottle and the sandy nook of puke on the doorstep welcomed me home.

13

Dear today, where did yesterday go? Lying under the covers. The same all over again, right? Give me a break. Bending to the waning crescent of the day, my lazy morning scrolling session, refusing time's natural flow, was interrupted by a call from Samira. She told me between fits of laughter that Keshav's scene was removed from the final cut of the pornographic film because he didn't suck the tit convincingly enough. Those milky-white breasts, well-shaped twin rosebuds, fair beyond other flowers, he could have done better. Stepped out for my silly little single-origin espresso and was met by a homeless man on my doorstep asking for money. Unfortunately my boyfriend pays the rent, you'll have to ask him. He didn't move. Checked my bag. No cash, sorry. What about something to eat? he asked. He had an Irish accent. Alright then. We walked to small Tesco, and for the length of time it took, he told me his life story. But it was a lot, and my brain doesn't work so well before a morning coffee. We arrived. What do you want? Cigarettes. Food? No, cigarettes. Fine. A £30 pack of tobacco, but what the hell. He thanked me and offered his elbow to bump, rather than his hand for a shake, because it was covered in dirt and sores. We both said have a nice day.

Thereafter everything about the day was dull under the spilled milk of blank sky. Silent sound space in my blank mind. My lungs filled the page. Overcast but with no clouds, life drained from the city. Absolutely nothing inspiring happens in London when the sky looks like this. Emails were answered. The heat soon became intolerable. It warranted a quick trip to the air-conditioned Prince Charles Cinema, where vegetable cinemagoers were planted in their rows before the house lights dimmed. The screen played David Lynch's *Lost Highway*. The hottest woman alive saying *you'll never have me* during sex is nasty work. No wonder the guy drove off a cliff. Then, *Inland Empire*, although the new restoration didn't make much sense. Didn't Lynch shoot the film in low-res to give the effect of pornography or a surveillance camera? The restoration probably just gave momentum to the rerelease. Grasping for what we can get. Hollywood has become a tired entertainment-industrial complex churning out corporate films.

Jump-cut thoughts. The art world is dead corporate, too, although it didn't used to be, something you really notice in surrealism exhibitions, when being weird was normal. Caleb hates surrealism. He thinks it's too gimmicky. It is only at surrealism shows that Caleb reaches the exit before me. We never walk around exhibitions together. We have a different pace, plus it's work for him, so it becomes his experience, with me tagging along, constantly aware of his ways of seeing, following his gaze. However, he is useful whenever there is a particularly inaccessible artwork, because he can explain how to look at it. But otherwise, we usually just discuss the work afterwards over coffee. After the David Lynch double bill, under the surgical lights of Joe and the Juice my lips sipped at the soggy paper straw of a pressed kale gastric juice. Skipped the long queue, the original modern sin. Eyes taped themselves vacantly to the wall then a book. Read Darcy O'Brien reading Flann O'Brien. Nausea *du jour* is passively consuming.

Joined the long queue for a salad bar just to feel part of something. The pencil skirts behind me discussed their weekend in the country and their office discount at a luxury spa in Saint-Tropez. This type of woman has the most uniform social identity in the city. Is there a way to be a successful thirty-year-old woman in London without a beige Burberry trench coat? Sat rheumy-eyed on a doorstep and ate my salad. The meridian of the afternoon is intolerable, when nausea rises with the realisation of a wasted day. Paralysis, under a dun sun in a dead sky. Float in the bath, Ophelia. Two icebergs jutting from dirty bathwater like knees. Didn't Clytemnestra kill her man in the bath? Scroll until the time notification appears on all social media apps, amplify your dull anxiety. Listening for a notification, waiting for a sign. The internet used to be a way to escape reality. Now the offline experience has become a way to escape the internet, which is perpetually staining vision and blotting out reason.

Waiting is the gaps between the numbers on the clock. It's the same nausea that Sartre described in *Nausea*. Imagine, in the olden days, before even mediaeval brick phones, people would leave the house to meet a friend and just hope they turned up. Motorway veins clogged with Fiat 500s, not knowing whether they'd make it on time. Pure waiting, like at bus stops without the live electronic arrival times. Maybe staring at raindrops on a glass window or physically writing a shopping list with a pencil and some paper. Or leaving a voicemail. Gen Z don't listen to voicemail. Texted my aunt in Beirut. Asked what her biggest insecurity was as a young woman. She said there was a war, so she didn't really have time for that.

Today the day is all the same to the clock and much the same to me. It is impossible to enter a deep state of thesis-editing focus on restless days like these, as if just sitting down and doing it was the most difficult thing in the world. Biting my pen, beating myself up. Sentences fall on the soul like dew on the pasture, on this same flower who smiles today and tomorrow will be dying. Perfect smile, sponsored by incense and myrrh. Too overwhelmed by literary lines to take a step forward. The thorn diadem, the wave of vomit, the appeal to outside pity, the re-entry into the human family, the sponge landing with a repulsive squish in the centre of a boxing ring, flung projectile into the arms of an easy reconciliation. There is an angry star governing me. Get yourself hung up and reel off requiems. Thought with fondness of the small sugar-loaded cakes from the Connaught. Except they don't have any vegan gluten-free options. Nor does

Marchesi, across the road. Violet's have a vegan and gluten-free chocolate cake every second day. My mum loves the tahini brownies there. Violet's have mums in a chokehold. It's the new Cath Kidston. By the time this finally comes out, we'll all have reverted to drinking real milk again, but that's unlikely under capitalism, forever presenting us with more products. Has consuming cow's milk become anticapitalist? Our bones have become as brittle as preconceptions. The London Fields diet is popping shitloads of pills but refusing to drink cow's milk. Elsewhere in the world the girlies come and go, talking of Ferragamo.

Nausea is a symptom of being freelance or working from home. Pay cheque to pay cheque has nothing on invoice to invoice. You lose all sense of national holidays. You forget about Guy Fawkes until you see fireworks on the walk home. Simultaneous restlessness and paralysis permeate the city, a condition tourists mistake for energy. Always outside, a pro in the public. Emotional anaemia is avoidable if you develop the foresight to run to the nearest coffee shop and surround yourself with other people fast. There's a new coffee shop near me which doesn't even serve coffee. It only serves adaptogenic lattes. Why not? So much of modern café culture makes no sense anyway. When people at cafés say watch my stuff, what do they mean exactly? If a hypothetical rogue entered the café and tried to steal their stuff, are you expected to chase after them? E5 Bakehouse serve the best vegan pastries. The pure joy of an upturned Gore-Tex bucket hat if they manage to secure a table at the Dusty Knuckle or Pophams on a weekend. There is great coffee at Pavilion, although the paper lids are annoying, and at Climpson & Sons, but they only do takeaway, like the bakery on Redchurch Street whose logo is a childlike scrawl. There's a spot on Curtain Road that offers the most alternative milk options and has crucifix wallpaper. Discovered a good coffee at a Japanese café in Spitalfields, but it's not a laptop spot. If you use your laptop in a nice coffee shop, they make you feel like a second-class citizen. There are many laptops at WatchHouse-esque cafés, but those places feel too much like corporate offices. The architectural lobotomy of a new build. Normalise funerals for dead laptops. It's like losing a pet, given the amount of time we spend with it. Even if the shiny new one looks exactly the same, you can feel, the lack of files. It's not the same. In a crowded London shop / An open book and empty cup, wrote W. B. Yeats, who would have been another speciality coffee shop fiend.

There are only a few coffee shops in the area that stay open past four o'clock, such as Blank Street or La Bouche on Broadway Market. For some reason, this is the time when people are supposed to stop drinking coffee. The coffee spot that feels most like a treat is Nobu Café in Shoreditch. They do the best matcha latte, that syrup-green Lethean ooze. It feels like a treat only if you limit your visits, such as after completing some menial task you didn't want to do. There is good matcha from a spot in Spitalfields, which also has a branch in Selfridges. My mum used to take me to Selfridges to see the Christmas window displays. Selfridges is now the annual destination for my last-minute Christmas shopping, with hourly matcha breaks to calm the nerves.

If your anxiety prevents you from leaving the house and it is past four o'clock, then a quick way to calm the body is napping. My hands handled themselves in a remix of 'The Ballad of the Lonely Masturbator' by Anne Sexton. O Anne, Anne, with a dead box of stones and spoons. It is around this time that horniness and fantasy collide. Scroll through camera roll for old selfies to post, edit photos, numb the brain. The only certainty in states of dissociative anxiety is the weight in the pit of the stomach and the suspicion that something is not going well and perhaps never has. The clock passes midnight, which produces premature feelings of anxiety, because you need to wake up early for work. To arise and work now, go not to Selfridges.

Maybe now is a good time to work? But of course if you were nauseous at four in the afternoon, it is impossible to focus at night. Your mind is occupied with far more pressing questions. Does a lobotomy remove forehead wrinkles? Is Tracee Ellis Ross a lesbian? Who named Earth? Why do Jamaicans love Celine Dion? Is Taylor Swift a descendant of Jonathan Swift? Benefits of double cleansing? Which bird can fly the highest? Is Ibuprofen or Paracetamol better for period pain? Is retinol actually good for you? Is Nicolas Cage a Coppola? And so on, until you work yourself into exhaustion, which brings about a deep sleep. Close your eyes, which are a secret.

Nausea can also arise from anticipation when the entire day has been spent waiting. The worst thing about having something fun planned for the evening is the knowledge that when you reminisce about that particular day in the future, you will remember only what happened at night. You wake up knowing that whatever happens during the day will be utterly meaningless, unless you do something remarkable. You need to keep up because tomorrow will only be faster. Brooding day anticipates raucous night with dull disdain. Those are often the days when you feel motivated to make either great or terrible decisions, like booking a flight for tomorrow to Marseille to write a novel that will justify all of the hangovers. This will probably pass with age, even though being twenty-three years old feels so old already.

My feet trundled to a favourite restaurant in Mayfair for a double espresso. The restaurant feels like the inside of a boat and is located opposite the Stephen Zweigler gallery, where Evelyn sits lonely in her lighthouse or townhouse awaiting drifts of gossip. Sometimes she will spot me through the window beside her desk, behind a noiseless, completely silent curtain runner, and join me for an orange juice. She spotted me. How is your summer going? Evelyn asked. Summer is . . . Waiting for myself to become myself again. My acrylic talons damage my actual nails. It's a pain getting infills anywhere outside London. None of the nice hotel establishments have anything to do with fake nails. And only a few hotel bathrooms have the detachable diffuser hairdryer head for curly hair, such as Cour Des Vosges Paris and Hotel Grace La Margna St Moritz. They have them at Third Space Islington, but not Third Space City. My fake nails: very long, very pointy, OPI Big Apple Red. Several respectable women in the art world have asked how it is possible for me to masturbate. Evelyn advised me to start taking Biotin to strengthen them. Someone else advised me that one must absolutely not take Biotin for nail repair because the pills have a plastic sleeve. If there is one thing people in the art world have strong opinions about, it's pills.

Another restaurant in Mayfair to waste time in is a relatively new spot which is super flashy and camp. It's exactly the type of place where you can observe Birkin bags having lunch with Dunhill derby shoes away from the prying eyes of housewives and househusbands. There is leopard print everywhere, on all the cushions, the bar stool upholstery and even the carpet leading down to the lavatories. They make cocktails with giant ice cubes to be slugged by elderly women who don't remove their giant fur hats during meals. Knock-off Audrey Hepburn in *Romanian Holiday*. All of them old enough to remember MTV. It is also the type of restaurant where you can spot some waitresses searching the guests online. In Elgin House, some waitresses allegedly follow the guests upstairs. Stories of naïve young women following and unfollowing and following and unfollowing their one-night lovers, hoping they will be noticed among the hundreds of thousands of other followers, as if that's the reason they aren't being followed back. Eating in the same restaurants each evening is important to turn city life into village life. Having to decide where to eat each night from the thousands of restaurants here would take up valuable work time. Cosmopolitan anxieties have been immortalised in masterpieces such as Federico García Lorca's *Poet in New York* and early seasons of *Emily in Paris*. When you begin to live a comfortable life in the village of the city, a flattening of experience can occur. This novel is being written on the precipice of my curiosity, before it migrates elsewhere soon.

There was another evening and another art dinner. These dinners happen almost every night, but they take a lot of effort to organise. Sometimes months, in the case of fund-raising galas. There have already been a few galas this year. Bottega Veneta invited me and Caleb to their table at a museum gala, but it coincided with Cannes Film Festival. We were on their table at another gala. Julianne Moore sat opposite me, and we asked the waiter for more bowls of crisps during the mime act. The high prices of gala tables, the auctioned artworks and the smaller financial pledges to educational programmes often add up to huge sums of money. The auction part can be very exciting: you put your hand in the air and make a bid, and then if someone wants it more than you, they raise their hand and then the auctioneer keeps raising the price for the artwork until the hands stop going up. Going once going twice sold. This stresses out Caleb because my hands throw themselves in the air for the fun of it. Fingers burst from the palms like flowers from a branch, exercising their autonomy. The most exhilarating gala auction this year was at a museum in New York where a legendary video artist mirrored my gleeful gesticulations as if we were on a rollercoaster, competing with the people on a patron's table who were actually buying the art. Apparently it's not allowed, what we were doing. There's a term for it. Can't remember. Auctioneering is an art form. Leila's husband organised a gala hosted by the senior auctioneer of contemporary art at a major auction house, who was funny. It takes a certain type of person to convince others to spend thousands of pounds over a plate of unseasoned chicken.

Another unacknowledged art form is the art of dinner table placements. It is always unclear who does them, but it is an admirable and invisible form of social labour which requires a vast amount of knowledge of the gossip and who's who in the room. Kudos to whoever invented double-sided placement cards. The placement gods put people together who already know who, or who would like to know who. Each person brings something different to the occasion, and it is a skill to be able to identity what that is and who will benefit most from it. At tonight's particular dinner, the placement gods seated me next to two who's, who were already acquainted with this who, but who didn't know each other. This who introduced those two who's, who got along brilliantly, each who already being a big fan of the work of the other who. Just a month before, this who went to Biarritz where a bunch of us had an evening swim in the rough waves of the fish-faced sea, in the Bay of Biscay, combing the white hair of the waves blown back. When the wind blows the water white and black. Caleb can't swim and watched us from a safe distance. We all slugged fruity cocktails and smoked and gossiped in the sluttish sea slush of a beach bar until closing time. An artist smoked pot through a hole in an apple. When Ovid wrote 'Beach Body', he wrote it for her. Kill all mosquitos. The dinner was spent reminiscing about Croydon with a British figurative painter, whose brother used to date girls from my first secondary school. She told me that Croydon was initially created in the 1950s to rival Manhattan, which is hilarious. Online, you can find old architectural maps of Manhattan/Croydon. It was a fancy event, but Caleb wore grey joggers and a paint-splattered t-shirt, the easiest way to identify a male painter in any room. He wears his t-shirt sincerely. Collectors, mainly people working in tech, have started wearing t-shirts instead of suits as a form of performance, a disappearing practice, a way to say: we're just like you.

Thank you so much, have a nice day.

Said goodbye to all the adults and jumped in a cab to an opening at Teddy's gallery. It was an exhibition of photographs and the penultimate show in his fishmongers. He is soon upgrading to a bigger place, a car garage just around the corner. The cab driver engaged me in conversation and tried to pin down my weird accent. He has correctly guessed the accent of every single passenger since he started his job three weeks ago. He said he hasn't ever travelled but spending time with so many international passengers has enabled him to travel vicariously. He the poet who kissed the lips on his palm. Arrived at the gallery and the crew was already there, plus an older man in a suit, an Italian dealer who recently set up a gallery in Lisbon, where there isn't such a big commercial gallery scene. Quite a few dealers have opened galleries in cities outside the regular orbit of the commercial art world, like Athens, Beirut, and Lagos. They are building infrastructure rather than just trying to break competitively into already-existing local markets. Most dealers make conservative decisions under financial pressure;

few are taking a risk to build new systems and structures. Instead, many young dealers in London leave their positions at mid-tier or blue-chip galleries to establish their own trendy spaces, and these new ventures typically function in much the same way as the places they sprang from, even working with similar artists. Some of the new galleries populating London include:

Asquire, Brooke Bennington, Brunette Coleman, Castor, Chemist, Collective Ending, Cooke Latham, Darren Flook, Des Bains, Dinner Party, Dovetail, Gathering, Ginny on Frederick, Grove, Hot Wheels, Incubator, Indigo+Madder, Lungley, Mackintosh Lane, Mamoth, My Galerina, Piccalilli, Pipeline, PM/AM, Project Space, Public, Qrystal Partners, Rose Easton, Sherbet Green, Shipton Street, Sim Smith, Soup, South Parade, Sundy, Vardaxoglu, Xxijra Hii, Young Space.

It is likely that some of the galleries on the list are no longer new, and by the time this novel is published, there will be an entirely new list. It's like a horse race. Only time will tell which galleries make it to the finish line. What definitely won't last? Vapes and NFTs. My bet is that Gremlin will become one of the next blue-chip galleries in London, and that Teddy's joint will become an important on the mid-tier. Gremlin are soon opening a second space, further down Shoreditch High Street, and they will build an artist's apartment on the top floor where Mary Jane Kelly, the final victim of Jack the Ripper, lay ravaged in her casket.

There is a turn towards artist-run commercial galleries like O'Flahertys in New York and site-specific projects outside the white cube, as delineated by Brian O'Doherty. The white cube, a virgin space that the art makes dirty. Many galleries have shut down recently, like JTT in Tribeca.

In London there is a new Bloomsbury group of galleries, surrounding Museum Street, and further down Theobald's Road. The young people who open galleries are typically from well-off families, and already have access to some sort of collector base. Buy low, sell high. Bad girls do it well.

Our epoch is one of art newsletters and art podcasts. People don't read news anymore, just the headlines. There are a few fresh art publications that speak to this resurgence in commercial galleries, stocked at Tenderbooks, Reference Point, and the independent art bookshops surrounding London Fields. London Fields is like Chinatown for Australians. Spicy marg women on dates with men dressed like toddlers. Greasy paper bags of almond croissants in one hand and oat flat whites in the other. Mortgages in Walthamstow. Housewives in stripy t-shirts under maternity dungarees. Tennis. There's something inexplicably Freudian about a man sitting in a highchair. The run clubs are the worst. Seeing them while walking hungover to grab morning coffee feels like being on safari. Still, there are multiple kinds of run clubs, like different sects in the same religious belief system. The proliferation of new galleries follows a similar logic.

Teddy's opening had already climaxed. Alright you lot, where do we go next? Unfortunately home was not an option. There was a photographer taking installation shots, which are the new backshots. Everyone agreed we had to find air-conditioning, inner-city heat is stifling. The parked cars blurred in silver heat. The only seasons left in London are Autumn/Winter and Spring/Summer. Tom went to buy me a can of Smirnoff and Coca-Cola at the off-licence because there was an alcohol purchasing ban for anyone under twenty-five. The man behind the counter had asked for my ID and then confiscated my can, which is only the second time in my life that something has been confiscated. (The first was my copy of Mahdi Amel's *Arab Marxism and National Liberation* at arrival security at Riyadh Airport.) Speaking of national liberation, sexual intercourse between Caleb and me once occurred in the bathroom of a national museum during a grand dinner in their Rubens Room. We bumped into Teddy's part-time gallery assistant at the off-licence, buying four vapes. His name is Eddie, and he grew up in Hoxton, where his dad runs a small pet shop. Told him about the Vladimir Sorokin novel where the characters inject goldfish into their bloodstream to get high. Eddie recently sold me three goldfish, a surprise for Caleb and the pond in his new building. What did you name them? Baudelaire, Verlaine, and Mallarmé. Verlaine proved too sensitive for an outdoor pond and was relocated to the water dispenser. No-one wanted to drink goldfish water, so the water dispenser became an installation. Numerous curators came on studio visits, and they would stop to watch and comment on Verlaine's performance. Eventually, a collector bought the installation. The other goldfish didn't have such an illustrious career. Baudelaire died a natural death, which won't be expanded upon. But he wound up deader than the Turner Prize. Soon after, the tomb of Charles Baudelaire, so Mallarmé writ, became a soil mound, soiled by a fox, and Baudelaire's carcass was consumed by a neighbourhood cat. Shit.

Tom told me to bring my sexy Parisian friend along. Which one? The son of the Peruvian Maoist. We commissioned Keshav to distract all the other guys who wanted to get with the dish of the day, but of course Keshav and the sexy Parisian left together at the end of the night. One expected a future, and the other expected a night, so none of it lasted more than a moment. Tom confronted Keshav. Jesus did not die on the cross for you to be a hoe, Keshav. Ngl, Tom's right. Keshav has seen more helmets than the Normandy beaches. Keshav is in an open situationship, but really it is just a bad relationship. Keshav has a coat of arms, you don't, Teddy told Tom. Tom dislikes the whorish whirlwind of the gay scene. He finds it unpleasant. The same mildly unpleasant feeling as when you've just showered but are in a rush and end up running outside with a shirt damp from your wet hair. Anyway, Tom got plastered and spent the night talking about his younger brother who had committed suicide. The brother had inherited Tom's coolness and signed his suicide note with a star-shaped pimple sticker. What was the point in killing himself? He was too cool to have a point. Is it that uncool to have a point? Yes, that's my point. For Tom's thirtieth birthday, Oscar tried to summon his brother's spirit in a scatterbrained séance with scented candles but, failing in that, did manage to arrange an obituary for him in an art publication. Hey, Tom, were you alive when they had to manually change clocks? What? Wait, Oscar, where's François? Who? Um, that guy you made us hang out with all night at Dérosian? Oh, him . . . People fall off. He thinks we hate him because Romy still hasn't followed him back on Instagram. The Doig sisters suggested we go to a pub near their home. This was a better proposal than the Weatherspoon's beside the Barbican that Teddy loves, where someone once got fatally stabbed with a fork.

The exhibiting artist was far chicer than Teddy, which represents the paradigmatic difference between European and British gays. There are also many Austral gays in the art world, but they usually disguise themselves as European gays. Teddy's ideal assignation would be Nando's for dinner, followed by *The Little Mermaid* at the Odeon, and then Simmon's for a cocktail in a teacup. Peri peri peripatetic. Teddy used to perform for his parents each evening, so he could go to bed with applause. People's parents are often better than people. European gays in the art world are fancy-dinner-at-Blue-Mountain-School-with-the-daughter-of-a-shipping-magnate. Teddy's exhibiting artist once hosted drinks on their rooftop, where this narrator got plastered on spirits from a monastic distillery. Celestine and Carthusian and Carhartt. Pray, Olafur, eleison. European gays will ask you questions like . . . Is that archival or new season Prada? There is only one correct answer, apparently. Archival. It takes more time and effort to source an archival item. Which they would call a piece. Like a piece of shit. With archival fashion, you need to know where to go and what to look for. That means you just don't have, well, money. Style isn't about having money, it's about having personality. And apparently thrifting helps you achieve that.

Men like Warhol's interior designer boyfriend Jed Johnson are the blueprint for European art-world gays. Generally, European art-world gays are more serious and discreet, with pretentious and unspoken rules on what is considered chic. For example, one may only attend art fairs if one is invited at 11 a.m. on VIP day. One must not participate in art-fair traditions like shoplifting from the Gail's pop-up. One must not go if one is not invited and one must never pay for a ticket. Paying means you're not *really* in it, and people will know. Wait, some people pay to get into art fairs? These European gays are extremely active online but only post sophisticated, tasteful images of interiors and furniture. The historical section of an art fair is chicer than the contemporary section and there is far warmer lighting. It is only considered chic to go to a fashion show if you are flown out and dressed by the brand or friends with someone on the core team. It's better to not be invited than to sit on the second row. You must not accept every invite, unless they all involve a country house. It's better to be in the centre of attention rather than the centre of attention. Etc. The gay young boys enjoy the sheen of ivy best, wrote Horace, my Roman Empire. These codes are all amusing and funny to observe. There are also certain elegant things you can do if you are not a gay European man, like use a china teapot, wear luxurious pyjamas, and open an envelope with a knife. Wrap your tongue around a vocabulary of entrées. Frenchies are chic, Teddy admitted. But we're *cool*, Tom replied.

Sat outside the quaint pub munching whitebait and gazing up at the full moon peeking from behind the Shard. The Beckettesque protagonist in Mike Leigh's film *Naked* said he preferred to howl at the moon rather than visit it. True. My feet inappropriately touched London's pavements. The musky odour of the artist's e-cigarette mingled with the faint smell of dandelions in the pavement cracks, weeds watered by mayonnaise. Throw a dandelion into the sky so high that it will not come back. Baudelaire once described the flâneur as a botanist of the sidewalk. Diet cigarette smoke travelled upwards, incense ascending from the altar of the world. Most people in London will have a cigarette to relax instead of just taking a breath, which is why British people have awful teeth. Sniff a line from that Samuel Johnson poem about London whilst a bisexual talks you dead. Bartenders shook shakers between their hands, and we all did shots with them. My mouth ate fish and chips with the help of my hands. The barman gave me a free bag of Tayto's. Ignored a curator who calls themselves an organiser. They organise trendy names, rather than artwork. Conversation was a dialectical fairytale turning from theology to philosophy in a parody of intellectual glamour. The past called us to love passionately, but now we need a revolution in thinking passionately. And so on.

Everyone shared stories of their sexual awakenings at Chariot's Spa in Shoreditch, before it was shut down. A paradise lost on Milton. Once his body grew into beardom, teenage Teddy took the train to the city and told his parents that he was sleeping over at a friend's house. In reality, he would traipse to Chariot's and bang a forty-year-old engineer who struggled to get it up. The worst thing about sex isn't when you don't orgasm, it's when the other person pulls your hair and you've just had it done. There's a distinct similarity in colour and consistency between men's cum and hair conditioner. And women's cum with hand sanitiser. The table, now drunk, debated: what is your favourite revolution? Tom answered the Russian Revolution because of *Anastasia*. Samira said the Haitian Revolution, although La Commune de Paris was a close second. My first adult book purchase was *War and Peace*, because it was the thickest one in Waterstones and it gave me value for money. There was also a very big book by Robert Musil, but the blurb said he hadn't even finished it. Anyway, *War and Peace* was a very grown-up novel that contained words such as *samovar*. Only a novelist truly comfortable with the size of their polo stick could use a word like that. Or a Russian. We argued over where we should go for a group holiday later in the summer. Oscar said Akon City. Tom proposed Yekaterinburg where the Romanovs were shot dead in a basement. Teddy pushed for Las Vegas. Summer in London is Bar Italia, Prince Charles Cinema and M.I.A. through wired headphones, on that we agreed. Stop amplifying queer voices, my ears hurt, said the artist, joining the screeching discourse.

The after-after-party was at a nearby gallery, because the gallerist's husband had purchased new speakers and wanted to test them out. The gallery was behind the McDonald's near Old Street roundabout. The already-overflowing party listened to the speakers while lying on beanbags and drinking mezcal. Florine's greyhound, Argos, sat on my lap, his paws arranged in a variation of the five ballet positions. He snored. The air was sweeter blown from his mouth than his nose. Oliver, like Oliver Goldsmith, 'An Elegy on the Death of a Mad Dog'. Dedalus would be a great name for a dog. Florine said she never undressed in front of her dog. Teddy yelled down the phone and dramatically rolled his eyes. It was either a collector wanting to sell back an artwork or it was another museum asking for a 30 per cent discount. This isn't Bargain Buy, honey, he said, and hung up. Tom said he shouldn't be such a bitch to his clients, but Teddy said it's part of his character description. Teddy can be a total bitch, but he's tender beneath the surface. Literally, because he has arthritic bones. He found out three years ago. We went to the hospital together and he cried in the cab home. Keshav distributed gummies, which got everyone the same way as William Burroughs at Le Parade in Tangier. Keshav told us about a boy from his boarding school who had overdosed on Maldon Salt. Turned away and spoke to the sound engineer about my thesis. He didn't listen but kept leaning closer, whispering how he wanted his speakers to seduce. There was one awfully maudlin bloke who spewed nonsensical sentences, all mimsy were the borogoves, and the mome raths outgrabe. We had no clue what he was saying. His friend was comatose on the floor, mumbling both parts of 'Je T'aime . . . moi non plus' to a blonde aristo with a pottery practice.

In the bathroom, a girl drunkenly touched cavernous nostrils to her reflection and smeared a gash-red stick of Isamaya Ffrench across heavily injected lips, discharging an air that was ruinous and urinous. She's on heroin, Teddy whispered. Tom once saw her applying foundation with an Escoda paintbrush. She had tried to make fresh pasta in the studio using a Cricut machine. Some new partygoers entered. He's a blue-chip artist with an unhinged internet presence, said Keshav, pointing to one of them. *Where*? Samira whipped her head around frantically. She was just about to text an Australian screamo musician on Tinder. Samira, he wore a Vietnamese farmer's hat for his Boiler Room set. I'm not asking for much, she said as she drank sadly. He's gay, said Keshav, pointing at the artist. We already fucked, he added. I washed his paintbrushes, and he came all over my face. Put that in your book. Keshav, he can cum all over your face, but he can barely finish a painting. Kim once said . . . Kim *who*? Kim Kardashian? Kim Jones? Kim fucking *Cattrall*? Be more specific. Kim Jong Un. What did he say? Ugh, both of you, stop. The artist was joined by another artist, from Brooklyn. Their paintings were too bad for brightly lit white cube spaces, so they began exhibiting in dimly lit basements. Within a year they made it onto some Power List. They're cool, said Oscar. Meaning? Between Dérosian shows they'll do a pop-up in a laundry room. Their derivative artwork is a decorative asset for any storage unit. Mediocre artists like them are necessary, so gallerists can persuade clients to spend as a gateway to getting their David Hammons. God, cynical much? A stylist pulled me into conversation. What's your retirement plan? he asked. To open a club and call it *Glamorama*. Saw you Irishmaxxing at the JW Anderson dinner. He got mixed up between JW Anderson and Loewe. It reminded me of when an heiress posted a photo of Oscar Murillo but tagged Caleb. The stylist had just landed a denim campaign. For who? Guess. Levi's?

The after-after-after-party spilled over to mine. It was relatively tidy apart from a sock thrown over a record player, and there were a few bottles of champagne in the fridge. Oscar brought Clonakilty sausages. Teddy's face was like a beet as he pried out a stiff cork. Teddy is an allornothinger who treats having a good time like a competitive sport. The annoying thing about such a sport is that where you *aren't* is always more fun than where you *are*. And if it's not, you don't know that. This gives Teddy a vibe of perpetual restlessness, like a fly who travels inside a car but soon begins hitting against the window, trying to get out. He sucked on his vape. We're at the frontier of civilisation, he said. And then his usual rant: art-world nepo babies opening galleries should invest more in performance and video rather than painting, since they're the ones who can actually afford to do weird shit. What's your biggest pet peeve? Samira asked. When people ask for a price list but don't buy anything. My biggest pet peeve is when cab drivers take unnecessarily long routes because they don't know where they're going. The perk of black cabs is that they can drive in the bus lane. But nowadays most of them follow online navigation apps, and you don't know if they are taking longer routes because they genuinely don't know where they're going or because they hear your boyfriend's accent so think you're a foreigner who doesn't know the city like the back of your hand and try to charge a higher fee. Omg Romy, stop. There was a random popstar in my apartment who put the stud in star-studded. It's not so random, Caleb said later. Everything just seems random to you now because you're not old enough yet to understand narrative. Whatever. Her lips were a landing strip for a song to take flight as her Ledaean body sang a swan song. She hung out awhile in the languid posture of pleasure.

Tom's long body began to sway metronomically. Tom, are you alright? Pissed, he slurred. Pissed annoyed or pissed drunk? Tom left early. Tom rarely leaves early because he gets anxious about what people say behind his back. He stumbled up Kingsland Road and in the vague air smelt sourdough bread through a busted nasal cavity. He began to cry because he was being so unoriginal again. Trample lightly with a serene look, weary the reader. When would he begin to live his own life and not some fraud of a fictional character's? He was a fictional character who wanted to feel something non-fictional. What if his character became more successful than him? Obviously that wouldn't happen. But still, self-doubt kicked in. He only cried because that's where the narrative was going, which made him cry even more. Tears from eyes lashed by eyelashes, his angel wings prevent him from walking straight. The rain lost its balance and fell, arse over tit. Everything is a lot from the people you love.

Meanwhile, there was a discussion on the subject of fiction between myself and Keshav, who lay on my bedroom floor smoking a joint. There is psychological depth to surfaces. The surface is not surface level. You don't need to *go inside* a character, which is a sort of literary fucking, to get something out of them. Everything is already out there. Just wait for the characters to show you something. For example, Keshav, the fact that you chose to wear a transparent Aaron Esh shirt today tells me more about your state of mind than if you attempted to explain how you feel. Not that you could do that without the help of a therapist. You sound like Miranda Priestly, he said. The scene where she speaks about the symbolism of the green scarf. You mean the jumper. Green scarf is *Confessions of a Shopaholic*. But you get my point, don't you? Fiction is obsessed with authenticity. It doesn't make sense to me why we try so hard to make our characters seem like non-fiction. Bloated backstories are corny. Maybe the characters want to have their own backstory, said Keshav. They don't because they're not real. You're not real, Keshav. Ouch. But you're as fictitious as if you were real. Even so-called authentic people with *no social media accounts* are memes of themselves. We are the stories we tell ourselves about ourselves. Readers shouldn't *have* to be convinced that characters in novels feel real. They're not. The absence of physical bodies in a novel makes everything even more unconvincing. It's different in cinema or theatre. However, you still get my mind, insofar as it constitutes my thoughts looking outwards, less inwards. Less my mind, more my eyes. Time to get back outside. What's *real* doesn't matter, we're all genuine fakes. Time someone freed fiction from the trappings of non-fiction. Each character is included in a novel for a reason. Just make them achieve their purpose. We're only here because the things that happen must happen to someone.

What's my name? Keshav asked. Your name is Keshav. Girl. Change my name. No, it's too late now, we're nearly at the end. Bitch! It will be confusing for the reader. They can handle it. Call me something sexier. *No*. Fine. Keshav sulked. What's my purpose, at least? Well, that's the problem with you characters. You, Teddy, Tom, Samira, and Oscar. You have your individual purposes, which are vaguely tied to career achievement . . . But together, you serve a far greater purpose in this novel. Except you're resistant to the idea of even being my characters. Exactly, you don't own us. Well, precisely. Being a fictional character myself isn't easy, at the same time as trying to find my own voice, and fictionalising all of you, who are simultaneously fictionalising yourselves . . . But we all form a *scene*, and that's your main contribution to this novel. Me, you, Teddy, Tom, Samira, and Oscar. It's in the title. We're best friends, bound together by our shared references, which means it's sometimes hard to distinguish who's who or who's saying what. And it's difficult to communicate psychological depth when you all have too much to say. The snappy witticisms mask anything deeper. Even if they're more fun than anything going on beneath the surface. But you're writing us, even though you're fictional? Yes, which makes you my problem.

And a lot of the time, you get in the way of my purpose, which, it has come to my attention, may have something to do with becoming a novelist. Which is exactly the thing you're making it difficult for me to do. Huh? Sorry. Getting second-hand stoned.

You are difficult characters to write, which is making it difficult for me to write. Sometimes the symbol of a transparent shirt is the only indicator of your psychological state of affairs. It just depends how much readers want to decipher, beyond the novel. For characters like Samira, for example, a cry for help isn't an existential internal soliloquy. It's literal crying, whilst bingeing the Bridget Jones film franchise with two tubs of Hackney Gelato. She tried therapy but fell in love with the guy after three sessions. Women thinking their therapist is in love with them is the same as men thinking strippers care about them. Women want to haunt. My hands briefly lifted from the page to gesticulate. And for the old-fogey critics who won't know any of our codes beyond their surface, this novel will only ever be a shopping list of names and drunk exchanges. But for those who know, for the girls and the gays, it will mean far more. We need new . . . Jesus Romy, my brain is too stoned for this shit. Fine. Go get me a peppermint frappé, will you? And while you're gone . . . Yes . . . How daft it is for novelists to try and give an illusion of access into someone else's mind, when we know where it's all coming from, really . . .

Keshav had disappeared and forgotten about my peppermint frappé, so let me turn to you. Are you also not sober? It doesn't matter. My novel is fiction, which is as tangible as the physical copy currently in your hands and your fingers turning the pages. Look at your index finger now: obediently waiting to perform its duty, for which you have never even been grateful! It performed the same task for every page of every book you ever read, without your gratitude. My generation would call that a toxic relationship. The way we use and abuse our index fingers. Your hands holding this novel are the same hands that may soon hold your genitals or whatever else you use to masturbate. And notice that you will manipulate them for the same reason you read a novel. To feel something. The extent of fiction's effect on your life just depends on the extent to which you will surrender to it. My voice will pause for the length of time it takes you to process all of this, which is probably as long as it will take for you to read this sentence. My voice is emerging, baby. Let's return to the kitchen and dance maniacally until dawn. Teddy is making everyone a morning coffee with holy water. Do you want one? The sunlight's dust streams lazily into the loft windows, resting on our young sweaty skin. Small feet stepped on waves of ancient daylight, bare toes warming in the rising sun reflected on the wooden floor. Yawning, we stumbled up to the balcony to watch the theatre of sunrise.

14

The sleepless nights have created a puffy texture underneath my eyes despite the thick application of snail mucin. My interior life had begun slipping away again. This time it's bothering me. There is too much outside, too much life. Constant action, little self-reflection, which makes activities feel pointless. Give me back my broken night, my cosy room, my solitude, my secret life. The swan song to W. H. Auden's lullaby of the hermit's carnal ecstasy. There was a hot storm outside and my clothes were off. A curious tree beat a branch at the window to see what it could see. Plants beside it wafted scents of amaranths up to the pleasant penthouse of Jupiter. Sat naked on a cold chair, and my skin stuck to the plastic. People make chairs not in the likeness of God but according to the average bodily proportions of the masses. Here is my desk where dewdrops pearl the bluebells. My feet used a gargoyle as a footrest, another body has become a museum. The headless Hydra moved my bowels and statuary gut full of shit. Rising and raging, and so is the brute desire in my raddled loins. Doing, a filthy pleasure is, and short, and done, we repent. Tell me again, tell me you want me then.

The only measure of time is the steady accumulation of bullet points in my Notes app. Life is so short, forgetting so long. Soon your time is going to be turned down, feel the scorn of the men about town, Horace forewarned. Placed a gaudy crown on my concussion and danced the wry dance which made my nipples rise like rye bread. The satyr Silenus at the Silencio Club. This is the portrait of the artist as a young woman, who is late for another exhibition opening.

Briskly my feet carried themselves to Liverpool Street Station. Gregorian chants blasted through my wired headphones, which gave everyone on the Elizabeth line the illusion of spiritual yearning. Felt the lingering throb of something last night that was quite enjoyable. The rosy sun burned sullenly above the underground tomb. Entertained myself on the Tube by guessing who would be who if this were a hypothetical Georgian period. Chimney sweeps were the most interesting people in those days as immortalised by William Blake. How the chimney sweeper's cry every black'ning church appalls! Underrated characters, chimney sweeps waited a whole era to be seen by Charles Dickens. If he were a dessert, he would have been a fruit and nut loaf. There is a meme circulating of Timothée Chalamet comparing him to a medieval leather shoe. The tragedy of new builds is their lack of chimneys, chimneys are devastatingly charming. Terracotta chimneys and shrubs.

Once all the chimney sweeps were identified, the next task was matching modern commuters with other historical jobs. The man in front of me was asleep. His body poured over the seat. Saw a bunch of girls with strong faces and linen outfits. Many of the edgy-looking girls in the carriage wore the Reena Spaulings look. The I-want-whatever-happens body and nothing-ever-happens face. Case studies: any of those Lower East Side actresses, mostly former child stars, who are around my age. Bred from the fabric of the city, now on Hedi Slimane's casting couch. Generations of laissez-faire lassitude. Birth was the death of me. Scared of death, so happy to be alive. Death's kiss leaving lipstick stains on Sartre's grave. Enough. The suits on the Tube are consultants, the modern equivalent of a slum landlord. In historical novels women always faint, which rarely happens nowadays. Where are the women who faint? Fainting, poking, and kite flying have become archaic, along with pince-nez and milk bottles. The Tube carriage rocked, abyss at the stern, the swiftness of the incline, an overwhelming passage of the tide, carrying hundreds of people without the need to know each other.

Seeing you, seeing me. Ernesto Sábato wrote a novel in 1948 titled *The Tunnel* about an artist's obsession with and eventual murder of the only woman who really made him feel seen. He curled his fists, she curled her hair. The simp bookmarked her before knowing her, simply because of how she looked at his work during an exhibition opening. He ignored all the other impatient spectators, indifferent and distracted. He found her months later and confirmed that she understood. You think how I think, he told her. And what is it you think? she asked in reply. I don't know what I think, but I know you think the way I do. He fell madly in love, even though she made herself unavailable. It helped that she was young and hot. He loved her, he could never stop loving her, he would love her unto death. Each man kills the thing he loves, apparently. He killed her and ended up in jail. See it, say it, sorted.

Another erotic drama of seeing is *La Belle noiseuse* by Jacques Rivette, a loose adaptation of Balzac's short story 'Le Chef-d'Œuvre Inconnu'. In the film, an oldish and successful male artist is visited by a young mentee, another male artist, who brings his cute girlfriend. The elder artist becomes desperate to paint the girl, which makes her boyfriend jealous, even though her boyfriend never painted her. The famous artist paints the young woman, and it becomes his masterpiece. They never have sex, but the act of him painting her is far more erotic than sex, and then the *merde* hits the fan because boundaries collapse. See, they sat and held hands, and it meant all the things it usually does for people in that situation. Skin touched between hands. His love was gone and his hair was grey. Creating clear boundaries is the condom of intimacy, otherwise the seed of desire can grow and disrupt stability and comfort. My love was sticky self-deceit and dirty games, moaned Rimbaud. Only words can be exchanged with others. They're the most you can give someone without giving them your love.

A tourist interrupted my thoughts and gripped my arm to stop herself from falling. The encounter left three light bruises the shape of fingertips which my arm carried all day. The relic of a weirdly sensual physical interaction. Tourists don't know that you're supposed to stand legs slightly apart to stop you falling. My legs are fine, they're not *Vogue* legs, but they do have working feet at the end of them. You can tell who is a Londoner on the Tube because they will walk to a specific end of the platform as they await their carriage. They will be nearer the exit, when they exit. People visiting from New York, Paris, Milan, or Los Angeles do not count as tourists because once you're from one major Western city, you're from them all. London! The Mecca of every young aspirant to fiscal distinction, exclaimed Samuel Beckett. Holidays in the commercial art world are reserved for the month of August, when everyone chases the sun, and then the first week of January, when everyone goes skiing. These are often relatively long holidays because the galleries close for three to four weeks. Life starts over in September. Pinch, punch, the first of the month, no returns. The train gunned from a tunnel into 5G zone otherwise known as the 'atmosphere' upon which everyone savagely refreshed. Disembarked from the Tube of my thoughts and strolled through Hyde Park's rose garden in an evening sun like a pink bottom, sub rosa.

All set for a leisurely time in Hyde Park. Hyde Park was choked with grass, and the grimy lenses of my Prada sunglasses made me dull-sighted, hiding the infinity pools of sadness that pupil my eyes. Smeared sunscreen over my arms like mayonnaise and thought about how sensuous the city can be on a swelteringly hot afternoon. Read Douglas Hyde in Hyde Park. Pigeons on the grass and ducks in the water. Nothing tits up, apart from blue tits, skywards. The sky changed with the pages of my book. Leafed through it under a tree. Samuel Beckett's novel *Murphy* concerns an Irishman in London who desires nothing more than to rest and look around. Samuel Beckett had shaggy eyebrows and the singsong cadence of a cordial voice. My literary voice is as stylised as my outfits, even if they don't match. If you saw me, you would not believe this voice was mine. Most don't.

Teenage girls lounged by the lake in bunched linens and rustling ruffles. Their softly fragranced hands held cigarettes, smoking to drive away the mayflies. Tangled grass, dreampop in poplin. One girl danced for a camera and her chin jutted out with attitude. She blustered in swan wind for a choreographed dance. A couple walked past, a man and a woman. She swung her giant Simone Rocha pearl bag as they walked, hitting it against his elbow as he edged closer without her noticing. She ignored him and he kissed her without it being anything more than his own kiss. A person is always a saint at the expense of someone else. The gap between them became the same as between a pair of eyes, and like a pair of eyes each was unable to see the other, but nonetheless came as a pair. Time is the space between people. Beyond them, an elderly white couple sunbathing topless. Their skin, prison of pores, rusted under the sun like the bottom of a copper pan. White people always take their clothes off in the sun, whereas brown people put on more clothes. She lay in the nest of his arm where another woman once rested, who must have got the ick. Knackered with the weight of a world that wasn't mine to enter, my eyes were distracted by two children playing. They were fishermen plunging plump fingers into puddles, trying to extract their image, kissing the delicate circles on the top of the water. He was free, she was four. Plagued by hay fever, my nose sneezed on snot-green grass. Eyes well and watch with wonder, weary of wars with the world.

My thoughts (and how privileged you are to know them) continued to jump around like bedbugs in this pillow brain, interrupted by arms that threw themselves timelessly around my neck and lips which kissed mine hard. Caleb's tongue flickered towards my mouth. It was difficult to see the flame whilst already cradled in the arms of the sun, whose shine fell with affection on his face. We smiled between kiss and kiss, all his flesh puckered into a mouth. He applied Vaseline as lip balm and looked at his reflection in the sunglasses sitting on my nose, using my star-freckled face as his mirror. His eyes were all pupil. My lips, a soft merchandise, with wild hyacinth woven through the hair that fell down my back. Opened front camera, my face looked rural and ancient like a rain-beaten stone. The road of his arm stretched from shoulder to forearm to middle finger to clasp my hands. Chatted some stuff. Unfortunately, we have great conversations, meaning that much of what *should* instead have been written down in this novel never was. We waded through the tall grass of bodies in Hyde Park. Surrounding us, men who wanted to grow hair on their bodies, and women who paid to remove it.

We strolled over to a museum for the opening of a monumental public sculpture designed by an Italian architect. By the Serpentine a myrtle tree caught my eye and cut the bark of my park poetry. Caleb occasionally spits on the side of the pavement when he walks, which is a character trait he invented for himself. Mine is humming like Glenn Gould. Our fingers interlaced to form a daisy chain. Hands undone, bent to look at our shadows on the dry grass of violet hour. Give me back my fingertips that touched you too many times. O my beloved touching his mind that no faithless counsellor can inflame. We arrived and snacked on Ladurée macarons, lightly holding them between translucent pads of index and thumb. Ladurée macarons have nothing on Jaffa Cakes. Bumped into a person who keeps pronouncing my name wrong, but it has been too many years for me to correct them. Networking is insufferable unless there is a genuine curiosity about what the other person is doing. It is so easy to spot whether someone is genuinely interested in what you are saying. There was a man trailing Emerging Artist #4. Old white men in the art world have a very specific kink for Asian girls. Emerging Artist #4 even wrote a Substack about it. Spoke to a *Tatler* editor with a Lulu Guinness handbag. She opened it to show us her new PR-gifted suctioning device. Arabella told everyone to buy a sleep-tracking ring because it changed her life. Bumped into a bald patch who told me about his new Netflix film whilst masticating a cigar. Some films are novels, like *Lucía* directed by Humberto Solás. Netflix and chill? No. *The Cremaster Cycle* and fuck. My vision strangled my tongue, infinity blared in my eyes. O Sister of Mystery, O Myth, O Misery.

People spoke to each other, and many were dolled up for the occasion. The best-dressed person this side of the continent is Bushra, thanks to the Zaha Hadid influence. She wore vintage Schiaparelli couture. To briefly sketch Hadid's wardrobe, her apartment was an expansive room of steamed translucent clothes bags that contained nothing but Issey Miyake. This made sense, since Miyake's silhouettes were architectural. All older ladies in the European art world wear Issey Miyake Pleats Please trousers. Their husbands wear Yohji Yamamoto–esque parachute trousers with wide-brimmed hats. RIP Zaha Hadid, you would have loved salmon sperm injections. There was a glamorous elderly Lebanese woman wearing a vintage Chanel suit which she had acquired just before the civil war. Her eyes were as brilliant as shop windows. The henna dye on the crown of her scalp looked like dried blood. What do you do for a living? My husband, she said. He was an impulse purchase, a himbo in limbo. She was accompanied by a young art historian who introduced herself to us as a culturepreneur. But she was just a Gmail art advisor, a lazy one, because she gets paid on retainer instead of commission. It's mainly American collectors who hire art advisors. Europeans tend to be more comfortable in their own taste. The Lebanese woman said America is perverse because it is built on the sentiment that people are free even though they are not. The American dream today is to leave America, she said.

There was a dinner after the opening at a wealthy patron's house in Soho, which was modelled on Cosmic House or Charleston House or Sir John Soane's house. It was their hosting house, not the house where they actually lived. The party was spread across opulent wooden tables in a medieval-style banquet hall, with antlers on tartan walls and thick solid instruments to pick up thin slices of carpaccio. An indie sleaze paragon performed live as guests slurped cold soup. The number of party guests was economic, much like the host. That's why he's a billionaire. That and arms dealing. To my misfortune a man named Raven parked himself next to me. Ghastly grim and ancient, he poured sweaty soup past thin lips. The odour that emanated from his armpits moved me to pity. He had that elderly Holland & Barrett smell. A tall, straight, white pillar of colonialism. Bring back the time when rich children were named after Farrow & Ball colours. Fanny, Prudence, Leopold. With double-barrelled surnames. Heavy on the dash. Romy, do you want children? No, gotta be productive before reproductive. The rosy-pink flame fluttered in my mouth and suppressed the yawns that pushed towards its roof. Raven spoke in his croaking voice about a small island, Nevermore, which he plans to turn into a golf club. Cupidity lending wings to stupidity. The most fun thing to do was crack open langoustines. A fat fly landed on the table and scrubbed himself all over. He moved his delicate forelegs like a person soaping their hands, occasionally brushing the top of his bulbous head. Slapped my palm down hard on his body. That's what's going to happen to the next person who calls me English.

My fingers toyed with a champagne flute, which looked even more beautiful empty. It's difficult to find meaning in life for people who are born with everything. It was always my secret, my aspiration for a beautiful life. If people knew how much my heart used to desire this life, they would think me extremely vulgar. During secondary school, Tumblr told us aspiration was American Apparel tennis skirts, JuJu Jellies, frilly socks from Topshop, Arizona iced tea, pastel-coloured Fujifilm Instax Mini cameras, Lana del Rey on vinyl, and Cara Delevingne on the cover of *i-D* and *Dazed*, purchased from a local WHSmith. The most iconic *Dazed* shoot was when Jawara Alleyne dressed Rihanna as a life-size blunt. Now, it feels more aspirational to reconnect with my original community and learn how to turn whatever this is into a craft.

There are occasionally academics at museum dinners, those sybarites of the suburbs, who are seasonal and unfussy like small-plate restaurants. The academics discussed their unfavourable views of AI chatbots. The artificiality of intelligence has made them anxious, probably because many academics are trained to think and write following a strict formula, which is essentially an algorithm and reproducible. I may turn out an intellectual but I'll never write anything but mediocre poetry, wrote F. Scott Fitzgerald in *This Side of Paradise*. The body is only a burial ground for the heart. What a load of type. Conversation was led by Mr Cogito, the foreign academic du jour with crystal eyes and violet gums and whitening hair. He said he was dating an older woman, meaning the same age as him. He was more American than a Donald Judd chair and spoke about the merits of democracy. My unpopular contribution to the discussion was that democracy does not mean good. For example, Israel is the only democracy in the Middle East. At the mention of Israel, the academics fell silent. Of course.

There are many problems with academic discourse today. In liberal society, language has gained an absurdly elevated status. It is used to police beyond any reasonable limits. Words are often conflated with real violence, as if they're as harmful as actual torture and death. Filling the silence thereafter, a bushy moustache asked in a polite tone whether it was in my interest to ever consider studying or going to university. Unfortunately not, my time is too busy spent sliving, drinking matcha, and toning without bulking. The men on the table nodded attentively, without catching my irony. Dull-minded, shaking my beautiful excuse for a brain. An elderly German art historian told me that my womb without a child would be like a museum without statues. It isn't my turn to bring people into the world, sir. It's only my duty to bring people to parties. Stood up and left to join Caleb's end of the table. Coughs, moans, and whispers bent over the long table, spluttering some collective hymn. The auto-icon of Jeremy Bentham would have been a more fun dinner guest. Enough, Catullus, of this silly whining.

A senior style reporter sat next to Caleb. She was recently tasked with deciding who would be *it* for the next cover of *British Vogue*. This was difficult because the publication had reduced its print run, so the chosen one would have to be *it* for at least two seasons. How's your mum's chemotherapy going? she asked me. Soft eruptions blew from my Skims shapewear upon eating a gluten canapé. There was a frustrated patron at their table who tried vainly to be included in conversation. She donates £50,000 each year towards the museum's acquisition of a new artwork. She is paying to be included and thus deserves to be included. More than me, at least, who is included in everything, but doesn't pay for anything. A nobody with a lot of body. A mid-tier dealer took this as the perfect opportunity to descend on the lonely patron. The mid-tier dealer moaned about the most successful artist in her programme, who she said behaved like a brat in front of one of her clients. He only turns it on for certain people, she sighed. Caleb's hand found mine under the table, that hand with a touch that collectors pay serious money for, which is a strange thought. Visual art is fundamentally about touch, so unlike writing. How or where or when my fingers touch my keyboard hasn't influenced the material of this novel.

Went back to my side of the table for the main course. The conversation had become a discussion of micro-dosing for focus. Meals were eaten by mealy mouths, lowered reverently to plates as if saying a prayer. Growing generations into my boredom, snuck out with Caleb to have sex. In the bathroom, we reached the point where my underwear would have been taken off, if there were any underwear on me to begin with. Wink. Caleb slanted inside me and cupped my ass with a palm like a psalm. My eyes rolled to the back of his head in pleasure. Redheaded women buck like goats, Joyce wrote on page number twenty-six of *Ulysses*. His fingers browsed what was inside. Do not deny what is animal in the animal. Gen Z don't have sex too much, which is the least Gen Z thing about me, along with my abhorrence of iced coffee. Doing it and doing it and doing it. No arrow of Cupid necessary. That's how Telemachus fell in love with the nymph Eucharis. Nothing is forgotten by the body quicker than sexual pleasure, leaving only an indistinct memory of it being good (or not good). Rejoined our dinner company. A yawn broke apart my mouth. It has taken us three hundred thousand years to create this network of lonely indifference, rooted in an excess of life. My boredom was exquisite and excessive. Raven's Gmail art advisor pulled up a seat. He said there were no Americans coming to the fair in London this year. Propped the moons of my elbows on the white cloth of the dinner table, rested my squishy cheeks on the hard part of my palms.

There was a more fun dinner afterwards, celebrating an artist and her museum exhibition, hosted by Burberry at St John. When we arrived, they made us wait downstairs for the already late dinner to begin. Picture me looking sombre, silly and pale, dressed all in black like the vocalist of an ambient music group. Dave Bennett was court photographer for the event. A hand of your own on one hip, another hand around another's waist, tilt your chin slightly downwards, smile without teeth. Flash. Move on. There is a common misconception that a good portrait has something to do with the technical quality of the image rather than capturing the essence of a person. My image is much better blurry. There was a celebrity's hairdresser on standby. Next to them, a celebrity who'd vanished into the capital letters of a headline. Burberry had sent uncomfortable shoes. Having kicked them off, my bare feet welcomed the cold stone floor. Colder than the ice sculpture of Bella Hadid at a perfume launch party. My body wore skin like a blanket, and sound slipped from my throat like a snake, serpentine. Plodded barefoot across St John, which amused the art crowd and horrified the fashion people. The two groups were segregated in the dining room, although some fashion designers double as art people. Are you all partied out? I'm all eaten out. Huh? As in, I've already been to, like, two dinners tonight. Wink.

The actors were all on the fashion side, including a working-class Irish lad who had just been cast in Martin McDonagh's new film. He was with another actor who told me he wanted to date a woman who felt guilty about her beauty. A YBA photographer sat on my left. He had travelled from the countryside for the occasion and kept talking about his dog, who had impregnated another local dog. He showed me a picture of the animal, leg cocked, consecrating a tree with Myrrh, pale sorrow for wet branches. He was currently reading Caroline Blackwood, an overlooked novelist about whom Bella Freud, sitting on my left, told us a bit more on account of her father's brief marriage to Blackwood. Female authors masked as socialites: Caroline Blackwood, Sybille Bedford, Ivy Compton-Burnet, Sylvia Townsend Warner, Rosamond Lehmann. He urged me to go online and order some of Blackwood's novels, then and there.

The YBA photographer commended me for reading magazines and going out, which he called living *offline*. What does that even mean? When we're offline, we're still online. My generation communicate in a way that's informed by the digital sphere, even when we go on one of those boomer writer residencies where they sever the internet connection. Having physical connections has become aspirational for your generation, the photographer said. Well, there's so much life in my life that there's barely any time to write it down. But my nights are never documented on social media. That wouldn't be chic. Maybe that's because you're dating a man in his forties, he said. No. People only follow me because they know me, not because of my half-arsed, irregular content. My life happens offline. If you know, you know. It's better that way. The same people will still be with me if social media dies.

Meanwhile, a fashion designer asked the waiter to remove the eyeballs from her fish and the carnations from the table, because they reminded her of death. Another fashion designer sat on the other side of the room. He is married to an actress from an HBO show who is going to walk in John Galliano's next Maison Margiela runway show. She performed the voiceover in Helen Marten's recent artist film. Why do artist films always have such long names? There was a model/activist on our table, a jejune *jeune* who did not mask her boredom. She came from Greece, had a thirst for knowledge. She wasn't engaging, just reacting. The placement gods accidentally sat her on the wrong side of the room. In fact, everyone under the age of thirty was on the other side of the room. They were mostly model/actor, model/activist, model/curator or model/book club founder. Model/activist means resharing infographics on Instagram. You can take a stand nowadays even if you're sitting down. The confusing part is why people need to identify as activists to engage in activism. The model at the table told me it is more powerful now to be a guest in the front row of a show rather than walking on the runway. All the new supermodels are the same age as me. We see each other all the time, but they never speak to me.

My friends on the cusp of serious adulthood were elsewhere. Oscar had begun his night at a listening room in Farringdon and ended it tweaking in the smoking area of Orion Business Centre, dragging the fags dragging on fags, he texted. He ended his night with Samira and Keshav at a rave tucked into a cul-de-sac somewhere in South London. Keshav and Oscar made out for the ninth time this year. Then Snake Keshav/KKKeshav abandoned everyone for a hook-up. He found a guy on Grindr to stretch and gesso his canvas and got bladdered enough to be indisposed for the rest of the novel. Oscar has been known to DM nudes to Blick Art Supplies when he is trollied, hoping they'll offer him a discount. An artist on the right medication can achieve anything. Teddy represents Oscar. Good dealers build worlds, not just lists of representation, and they're doing their first art fair booth together this year. Don't say the F word. What? Wait until September, at least. Samira became miserable after Keshav and Oscar moved on. She cycled home on a Lime bike and scrolled through summer wedding content and people trying to sublet their flats for three days. The new sound of the city is a Lime bike being activated. Du du du duh. Do you remember life before Uber? The next morning Samira was scheduled to be interviewed by someone from a major New York museum, regarding joining their publicity team. Applause. For a while we celebrate in minor strain, straining eyes at the sun. Samira didn't mind the idea of leaving London. Not my citadel, she said.

Tom and Teddy were at Elgin House with their actor crush, a chiselled ephebe and Jonathan Anderson's new muse. He is perfectly non-specific for an actor today. Tom wouldn't stop telling the actor that what he was doing was culturally important, referring to his gay high school TV drama. Running out of things to say, Tom then publicly declared his obsession with Millie Bobby Brown, who was completely unrelated to the actor but the only other person Tom knew under twenty. Say goodbye to Tom, then say goodbye to Tom lost. Looked up from my phone. Everyone in the restaurant had suddenly disappeared. Stood alone inside my novel. This is the happiest part of the book. It's just me. If this were a film, there would be too many people involved in the writing process, plus all the people paying for it would have a say in the creative decisions. This is all me. It's also a lot of you. It's us, whatever that means to you. Make notes during the throes of things and communicate with the world when it starts to become fiction. Fiction is the outcome of ripened distance. Sarah Lucas appeared from the bathroom. She asked the waiters to gather up the remains of chocolate donuts in doggy bags, and she thrust them into my hands, since none of the boneful models ever ate them. The night outside grew darker, and the inside grew brighter as a waiter turned on the white overhead lights. Sarah reminded me about my shoes, all alone in a corner of the restaurant. Good morning, midnight.

15

WhatsApp, 25 June, 16:00 GMT

ROMY HEDAYAT: Are you ready?

TEDDY PEARSON: Yes.

RH: Damien Hirst or Mike Quinn?

TP: *Marc Quinn lol. MIKE!

RH: Lol. Btw wtf is up with [redacted]?

FP: He doesn't give hand jobs, he gives hand careers.

RH: Go on.

FP: The guy I worked in the bookshop with at Stephen Zweigler was obsessed with him. He only ever asked for twinks to be sent to his studio . . . I'm saying nothing!

RH: Robert Diament or Russell Tovey?

FP: Robert. Would be more into BDSM, I think.

RH: Gwyneth Paltrow or . . .

FP: Gwyneth. I like her candles.

RH: Levi Dérosian or Stephen Zweigler?

FP: Levi. No kids, more inheritance.
RH: Maria Balshaw or Madonna?
FP: Madonna. Who is the other lady?
RH: Girls Aloud or Spice Girls?
FP: Girls Aloud.
RH: *Wittgenstein's Mistress* or *Wittgenstein's Nephew*?
FP: What?
RH: Hans Ulrich Obrist or Malcom X?
[. . .]
RH: You're really thinking about this one.
FP: Malcom X, because it's the right thing to do.
RH: Or Mr Big!
FP: Mr Big. My dream man. Literally exactly what I want.
RH: What about your fiancée?
FB: Oh, yeah.

WhatsApp, 26 June, 11:45 GMT

TEDDY PEARSON: It's 06:45AM in the Big Brother house.
ROMY HEDAYAT: You just arrived in Jamaica, right? Why are you up so early?
FP: Because Teddy just woke up and needs to answer Romy's questions to win more food for the challenge.
RH: We should stop messaging on WhatsApp. There is a direct correlation between success and people who use iMessage.
FP: Me or Arabella?
RH: Teddy!
FP: I'm being a menace.

RH: If you always give an answer then life becomes a test.

FP: Lana del Rey or Enya?

RH: Lana then. Enya now.

FP: Harrods or Selfridges?

RH: Selfridges, duh.

FP: Not very Arab of you.

RH: Selfridges have a matcha bar. Since you're no longer spending £400 a month on vapes we can go shopping together.

FP: Fantasy threesome?

RH: A father, son and Holy Spirit.

FP: It's boring to play this with you because you know everyone.

RH: I can't leave the house without bumping into someone.

FP: Is that the moral message of the novel?

RH: There is no moral message of the novel.

16

The final allegro follows the adagio like a sneeze. Blinked awake from a dream that told me to book a trip to Marseille and write a novel, this one. Marseille is a sun-flung location, and its sea has the solitude of the countryside, with nothing but the friendship between a pair of hands. Hopefully it will be possible to avoid the holidaying clout chasers from London or New York, whose cerebral lobes often malfunction. Will go to Marseille after my brother's engagement party, which he has decided to have in the Middle East, surrounded by family. There's a general heaviness in my family that wasn't there a few years ago, a sadness that's difficult to be around for more than a few days. I'm skilled at numbing myself to it in London. But the pain is always there, repressed at the surface, which produces a feeling that I would call my humanity. Mentally preparing to sleep on the floor with my cousins, under patterned blankets, with the fan whizzing. The same conversations: Inshallah you are married and pregnant soon, Romy. Inshallah? That's outshallah.

My heart craved something familiar that didn't feel like nothing and solitary experiences to heal the slow burn of endless small talk, which had become unbearable. There is a growing inconsistency between my past and present which has made me wary for my future self. Coming into myself as an adult, one of my biggest fears is that my comfortable life will create a dull complacency and dampen my curiosity. That will never happen, but it is worth making a note as a reminder. My body increasingly craves moments from my old life when certain things made more sense. Life chose itself when it became obvious that there would be a story.

The great eschaton before my escapade to the seaside: the sixtieth birthday party of a prominent YBA artist. She celebrated her last birthday with a small dinner at the River Café and some artists travelled to London for the occasion. Essence of orchids in her tumbled hair, a swallow hairpin at her nape, holding coiled tresses. Caleb drunkenly reached under the table during dinner. His cold hand came between me and my Calvins. This year she's celebrating with a party in the basement of Maison François. It was sunny, a golden hail beat down on the tarmac of the plain. Shimmied off a tiny miniskirt in the cab and pulled on more respectable shorts because a pitstop had to be made in Fortnum & Mason to collect a gift. No trouble was prompted from the doorman which, surprisingly, my outfits have warranted before, besmear'd with sluttish time. But the hamper was so large it covered my shorts and gave me the confidence of a man whistling as he cycles. My fingers plucked like a lyre the tired laces of unreleased but worn-out trainers, two feet beneath my heart. Everyone was already at the party. Caleb soon arrived from his studio. Tom is like me in spending much of his time hanging out with sixty-year-olds at events like this one because they're often more fun than people our own age. I enjoy how older people sign their names at the end of text messages as if sending a letter.

There was dancing music for the former bad bitches of the bacchanals, who were of amber and smouldering fuse, spinning like mythological Ixion on his ever-turning wheel of fire. A collector asked me and Tom to take him to a party that wouldn't give him back pain. The palms of his hands slept on the blades of my shoulders. He'd had an MRI scan, and the doctor took music requests, so the machine rocked from side to side blasting industrial techno. Apparently it was one of the most intense out-of-body experiences he ever had. We told him to come to Adonis. These bottomless nights are our exile. We reconnect with the club because nature isn't working. Lonely in the crowd and lobotomised at the club. Painters danced, drunk as skunks on turpentine. We pledged to love through all disaster. We ate prawn tempura and discussed matters of tempera. How do you make it? Eavesdropping in media res.

A gay icon with the souvenir of an East London accent sidestepped over to us. She was all done up before the night undid her, already ready for the next party. The people's princess, she still DJs every night. Youth is only ever a chemical insanity. These days, youth has become simultaneously younger and older. There was a war because Paul did not put the people's princess on the guest list for the Madonna concert. He invited Daniel Sinsel instead, a dirge for the departing day.

Madonna once had a British phase, much like the Lower East Side kids right now obsessing over the British indie sleaze era. Madonna moved here, dated a famous film director and faked a British accent. She was determined to join the arty farty crew because it's the closest thing we have to Hollywood. That's how she became close with Paul. One day, Paul said: Madonna wants to meet the locals. Everyone come over for tea. The club girls spent the whole day assembling their outfits and informing all their neighbours that they were going for tea with Madonna. But when Madonna arrived at Paul's place, she just spent the evening with her tongue in some guy's mouth, and all the girls stood in a corner pissed off. The aforementioned people's princess now knows Madonna enough to say, Alright Madonna? So when Madonna wanted to go to the Turner Prize, she introduced her to the winner, who she said nearly died from the experience. Something similar happened when yours truly drunkenly tottered over to Girls Aloud at a party and put on a fake Derry accent to ask if Teddy, a super fan, could have a picture. He said it was the greatest night of his life.

My chosen beverage of the evening was mint tea, but then the birthday girl insisted we do tequila shots, and then we all got plastered. Everyone spent the night sentimental. Eyes welled up and lips kissed my forehead and probably the foreheads of others with motherly affection.

The night drew to a close, and an artist sat alone in the corner wearing a mournful expression. He was transfixed by the scene playing out in front of him, the YBAs wildly dancing with each other. The waiters manoeuvred in lively steps, sweeping empty bottles and toothpicks into plastic bags. It was a beautiful scene, and both of us tried not to cry. Came now the sliding of tears down his face. They all looked so together, which made him feel so alone. He said he felt in between their generation and mine, and neither can be fully claimed as his history. The moil of my double decade filled me with a softness from starlight. Shadows on the dance floor, vagabonds of love and loss scrawled into history. We watched in the wake of readers who have already turned the page. Your eyes that are never weary of mine. The tableau in front of us made me feel slightly nostalgic, too, for an epoch when women were increasingly on the scene.

The narrator left her book, left her tomb, and followed the sound of something that disrupted her gloom. We danced together until closing time, under the sparkling disco lights. It was a film, or the end of a film, starring three generations of dreamers. Endlessness will be mine.

EPILOGUE

'I' return, a sudden outburst for the epilogue. My four-day writing retreat is over. I asked the YBF group chat how the novel should end. Kill off Keshav, Samira texted back immediately. Why does it have to end? Teddy asked. People get the idea, I said, and besides I don't want it to turn dark or start feeling too same-y. Oscar said that Samira should definitely kill off Keshav. Or I'll give him too many Percy Pigs, he added. Well, I can't die, said Teddy, I need to be in the sequel. There's not going to be a sequel, I said. I want to become a proper novelist. Shut up, Romy, said Tom. I think we just need to go on more nights out, he added. On that, everyone agreed. Fine, I replied begrudgingly. The thought of another month of daily openings, dinners, and parties made me want to throw myself from the top floor of the Harpo. I couldn't even bear to be in London anymore. I began to feel suffocated by my lack of expectations, the stifling of my ambition. Girlfriend of, my arse. I needed to withdraw. Hustle to disappear. Instead of trying to explain myself to friends over dirty martinis, I began to write it all down. I didn't like who I was becoming, I had begun to sacrifice something of myself. I had to win it all back, my right to myself. It punched me in the face when I realised just how many people become comfortable valuing a certain status in life more than their work. The more sedate you become at a young age, the harder it is to change. Then you begin to feel suffocated.

It took an accumulation of nothingness for something in me to snap. My interest in vapid social life fell off, as did my desire to fall into it. I put my finger on 'it' so many times that my finger buckled under the pressure. Went on my writing trip to Marseille and stayed with some girlfriends from Cairo. Swam naked in the sea. The spume of the waves was white noise. My friends sniffed lines mixed with sand. Sea seasoned with salt. Sunburnt bikini lines. Stoned with a granite grin. Lay old-fashioned on the rocks. Determined now to be more present again in my community. Pushing deeper, it turns me on. Something like freedom, the option of isolating myself again to think more clearly about the future. There is more tenderness and gratitude for the me who brought me to the sea. Apollinaire wrote: *you in Marseille among the watermelons*. The avant-garde of the present is figuring out how to better communicate our condition today. More canonical nonsense to force down the throats of students. Their student debt sentence.

Lay on the beach and looked outwards. Words are my home, and my tongue will always have the roof of my mouth. The Mediterranean drifted with the aimlessness of clouds, stretch marks of the sky. How are you? Tom texted. He was at home doing more of the same. I feel like I'm on the precipice of chaos, I said. The sweetest spot, he replied. I'm writing day and night, I said. Well, at least staying awake all night partying has prepared you for something. Ha, true. The sea is wrinkled. Waves, Romy. They're called waves. The sea waves: goodbye, Tom. I will burst forward and grow. Met the Muse, on her way out. She laughed out loud: Is it you? Fell asleep in the sun, like at the end of a novel.

I messaged the YBF group chat and told them that the research trip is over. I would be yapping an epilogue of my own. Sorry, no, not going to happen, Teddy replied. The novel is about how unhinged we all are, he added, it can't just end with fiction because you can't handle all the partying and Percy Pigs anymore. It's hot when you become stern like that, Samira replied to him. Adjectives modified the noun, cramping its style. Samira is entering her horny era, having just fucked a colleague with Tourette's thanks to her flashy new job in New York. I'm a dom-top art dealer, Teddy continued. No, you're not, I replied. You just want me to include that in the novel. If you were dom-top, you would be smoking cigarettes, like Tom. I always leave the party whilst it's still good. Case closed. I didn't want to obliterate myself any further. It took going from members' club to members' club night after night to realise that all I had was me. I myself, whom I refuse to sacrifice to any system which holds whiteness and wealth at its core. Being with myself is what makes me feel most alive. Writing this brought me back to myself.

I have played fool to the point of madness. 'Tis the last rose of Summer left blooming alone. The party's over. I've landed on my feet. Feeling alive isn't enough for me, I want to live. I don't aspire to lifestyle, but to writing great novels. One day, inshallah. Rome wasn't built in a day, but Romy was. Writing *Scene City* is when I've felt most alive, more than at any of the parties. I can choose which future version of myself to become. I choose the best version of myself. What was the outcome of this nothing? Best Friends and a novel, which are something. Keshav, what do you think? I asked. Deathly silence.

